SPECIAL MESSAGE TO READERS

THE ULVERSCROFT FOUNDATION
(registered UK charity number 264873)
was established in 1972 to provide funds for
research, diagnosis and treatment of eye diseases.
Examples of major projects funded by
the Ulverscroft Foundation are:-

- The Children's Eye Unit at Moorfields Eye Hospital, London
- The Ulverscroft Children's Eye Unit at Great Ormond Street Hospital for Sick Children
- Funding research into eye diseases and treatment at the Department of Ophthalmology, University of Leicester
- The Ulverscroft Vision Research Group, Institute of Child Health
- Twin operating theatres at the Western Ophthalmic Hospital, London
- The Chair of Ophthalmology at the Royal Australian College of Ophthalmologists

You can help further the work of the Foundation
by making a donation or leaving a legacy.
Every contribution is gratefully received. If you
would like to help support the Foundation or
require further information, please contact:

THE ULVERSCROFT FOUNDATION
The Green, Bradgate Road, Anstey
Leicester LE7 7FU, England
Tel: (0116) 236 4325
website: www.foundation.ulverscroft.com

WHEN SHALL I SLEEP AGAIN?

Eddie Martin is on the run from a mysterious incident in his past. But when he comes to the isolated little midwest town of Garwood, his problems get a whole lot worse. He becomes involved with Sylvia Webster, a young and beautiful — but completely amoral — woman married to Garwood's elderly doctor. Like a spider to a fly, Sylvia sets out to draw Eddie into her web of deceit and personal gratification. Once caught, Eddie becomes trapped in a series of murders — a spiraling nightmare that can have only one grim conclusion . . .

NORMAN FIRTH

◆

WHEN SHALL I SLEEP AGAIN?

Complete and Unabridged

LINFORD
Leicester

First published in Great Britain

First Linford Edition
published 2014

A catalogue record for this book is available
from the British Library.

ISBN 978–1–4448–2085–0

Published by
F. A. Thorpe (Publishing)
Anstey, Leicestershire

Set by Words & Graphics Ltd.
Anstey, Leicestershire
Printed and bound in Great Britain by
T. J. International Ltd., Padstow, Cornwall

This book is printed on acid-free paper

Dedication:
FOR SHEILA

1

The heavy truck moved along the hilly, dust-laden road through the hot afternoon. Apart from the truck and its load of timber, there was no other living or moving object in sight. The stillness and silence were almost tangible, and over everything the sun flamed down with a wearying persistency.

There were two men in the truck; the driver had a beefy, red face and a greasy, peaked cap. He was typical of a million of his fellows on heavy haulage. His face glistened with drops of perspiration, and his tongue occasionally made a lethargic moistening movement about his thick lips. His companion was a younger man, wearing only a dirty striped shirt and dusty trousers which had once been part of an expensive tailored suit. He carried an odd jacket slung across one shoulder, and frequently mopped his brow with a dirty handkerchief. He seemed impatient, for some reason. Now and then he glanced back through the small square window behind him, over the load of limber and along the interminable winding road they had just traversed.

The driver spat from the window and said, laconically: ' 'Nother fifty miles, son.'

'Fifty? Hell, won't this crate go any *faster*, Mister?'

The driver was irritated. 'If you don't like the speed Lizzie's travelling, hop off an' see if you can *walk* faster. Bums can't choose an' pick — this ain't a Pullman car. If it was, *you* wouldn't be on it.'

'Sorry. I'm grateful for the lift. Just impatient.'

The driver eyed him. 'Ain't running away from anything, are you?'

'For instance . . . ?' The young man's tone was hard.

The driver shrugged. 'Okay, son. Forget I asked.' He shifted his eyes to the road ahead.

The hitchhiker said: 'How about this town you're heading for? Midvale? What's it like?'

'Typical Midwestern dump. You know

— a Main Street, an' all the rest of it. Soda parlors, theaters, and a railroad station.'

'Small town — any police department?'

'Hell, sure. It's plenty big enough for *that*. They're mighty proud of their police in Midvale. Reckoned to be the top town in the state for absence of crime.'

The young man nodded thoughtfully and leaned back. The driver thumbed out a limp packet of cigarettes from his shirt pocket. He offered them to the young man, then took one himself. The blue smoke drifted lazily from the open windows into the oppressive atmosphere outside. The truck was nearing the summit of the road. The driver crooked his finger at a narrower road running off to the right.

'Leads to Garwood . . . '

'*Garwood?*'

'One of them small hill towns — a village'd be more like it. Pretty dead. About a thousand inhabitants all told. They ain't even got a *railroad station* there.'

'How's that?'

'Garwood's on top of a hill. No — *mountain*. The railroad company don't reckon it's worth the trouble to run a line that high. The folks there hardly ever commute anyplace, and they don't have any out-of-town visitors.' The driver grinned. 'Who'd want to go there?'

'Kind of — quiet?'

'All of that. They ain't even got a movie theater.'

'What makes folks *stay* in a dump like that, then?'

'They have to live. An' they ain't any great shakes mentally,' the driver, who considered he *was*, told him. 'Mostly they're farmers and sheep men. Do a bit of timber cutting on the side.'

They had reached the branch road and a worn wooden sign which said 'Garwood' which had a painted finger pointing uphill through the tall leafy trees.

The young man said: 'Thanks for the lift. You can hold her here. Garwood sounds like it may be interesting. This is where I get off!'

The driver stared at him. 'Huh? You're

nuts. Nobody *ever* wants to go to Garwood. Midvale ain't so much, but *Garwood* — !'

'That's okay. Stop the truck. This'll do me fine.'

The driver shrugged and obeyed. He watched the young man hop down and give a tug to his belt. He said: 'But you'll die of the peace an' quiet — '

'Just what I need. Thanks again for the haul. Sorry I can't — '

'Aw, forget it. I've enjoyed havin' your company. Why not come on to Midvale an' I'll stake you to a meal?'

'I guess not, thanks all the same. I'll be blowing now. So long.' He flicked his fingers from his head in a signal of departure, turned on to the narrow road winding up through the trees.

The truck driver watched him go; he didn't look back. He scratched his head and murmured to himself: 'Now what did *that* guy do, I wonder?' Then he lit another cigarette and started the heavy truck rolling again, away from the branch road and down the incline before him.

5

Panting, the bum paused for breath. The road wound up steadily in front of him, still surrounded by massive trees. He'd tramped for almost half an hour now, and there was still no sign of Garwood. He wondered if the driver had given him a wrong steer. But the road had to lead *somewhere* . . .

At every step the heat burned through the thin soles of his once-elegant shoes; a number of small stones had also somehow found their way in and were now digging painfully into his feet. He sat down and slipped both shoes off, emptying out the stones. He glanced longingly towards the cool shades of the wood at the roadside and wondered if he could make Garwood by taking a cut through them.

He left the road, carrying his shoes, and then stood on the soft grass at the edge of the trees. It soothed his feet. Then, with a last dubious glance along the road, he struck off into the woods, bearing upwards. He walked barefoot, reveling in the feel of the grass under his tired skin. After a time he lost sight of the road, but he held fast to his upward course. He was bound to break out somewhere, and it didn't much matter where. He had the rest of his life in front of him.

Off to the right he heard the trickling of a stream, and he cut away to trace it. It ran between two low banks, bubbling down the mountainside. He threw down his coat and drank from the stream, wiping his lips on the dangling sleeve of his unbuttoned shirt. Then he followed the stream upwards. Maybe it was the source of the water supply for Garwood. If he followed it he should be right. He doubted his ability to find a path back to the road now.

The going became steeper and the stream became a series of tiny waterfalls, tumbling and splashing over jutting, clay-like ground. He went through a belt of trees and entered a clearing which was taken up almost entirely by a fair-sized pool. It was surrounded by shady trees, with leafy plants growing down and drooping over the water at the edges. At one end a stream ran into it; at the other it continued its way down the mountain-side.

The water looked clean and deep. He draped his jacket over a fallen tree stump and removed his shirt; then, wearing his trousers only, he waded in and began to swim. Twice across the pool, and he relaxed and floated idly on the water, thinking. His thoughts were troubled, and gradually he became oblivious to everything but the necessity to keep himself afloat and to try to work out some of his problems.

Ten minutes or more had passed when the noise of footsteps crushing through the woods towards the pool made him come to a full awareness again. He waited a moment, undecided; then he moved quietly under the overhanging plants at one side and stood in shallow water, perfectly motionless.

Through cracks in the foliage he could see the owner of the feet making the steps. They belonged to a woman, whose back was towards him but whose figure argued that she was reasonably young. He had hoped she would pass without noticing his jacket. He had no wish to meet any strangers at the moment, especially in his present attire of water-logged pants, and with two days' growth of stubble on his chin. But she obviously wasn't going to pass.

Now he could see that she was slipping out of the light summer dress she was wearing. It came over her head and she hung it on a projecting branch to one side. Her slip followed; then the more personal articles of her clothing.

Still he stayed silent, hardly knowing what to do now. The woman turned at last, her hair streaming over her white shoulders. She poised beside the pool in a chosen spot, hands above head, ready to dive. Her body flashed as the sunlight struck it through the leaves, and arced in a white streak into the water.

She came up spluttering and gasping, swept the damp hair back from her face, and commenced to swim rapidly, moving with grace and precision. At intervals he caught flashes of her white body as it rose slightly above the water. At length she turned on her back and paddled lazily to and fro, hair streaming out on the surface behind her.

He began to feel uncomfortable. He wasn't in a cozy position, and his legs were already tired. If she stayed much longer he'd *have* to move. She showed no signs of leaving and at last he decided to put a bold face on it and make his presence known. What her reaction would be he had no way of telling — but he reflected that it didn't much matter, since they were clearly some way from any form of interference; otherwise she would not have been swimming nude so carelessly.

He slid forward and struck out towards her. She was floating in the center of the pool and didn't hear him coming. He was only a few feet from her when he said: 'Hello.'

She started, and then lost control and vanished under the surface of the water. He reached forward and gripped her smooth shoulders, helped her upright again, and held her whilst she coughed and spluttered wildly. Recovering suddenly, she knocked his arm away from her body and stared at him angrily. At this point the water came to her chin, and she stayed where she was, breathing quickly.

'Did I startle you?' he asked her.

'Why on earth didn't you choose some other way to make yourself known?' she snapped. 'And just how *long* have you been skulking here? You weren't here when I *came*.'

'I was — I hoped you'd leave again so that I needn't have caused you any embarrassment at all. But you didn't . . . '

He was seeing her features fully for the first time now, imagining them attached to the perfect body beneath the water, and his imagination was supplying a picture that made him suddenly hotter than he had been all that afternoon, despite the temperature of the water. Her face was small and prettily shaped, with full, enticing lips, inclined to pout a little. Her hair was auburn, her eyes green. There was a precocious dimple in one cheek, and about the whole of her appearance a suggestion of something

11

wild, strange and beautiful.

She said accusingly: 'You've been here — *all* the time?'

He nodded; he was looking for a blush, but there was no trace of one. And her anger was evaporating rapidly. She laughed suddenly. 'Hmmm. Well, what's the next move? If we wish to be very proper neither of us can stir from this spot, can we? But as you're the representative of the so-called chivalrous sex, I think it's up to you to leave *first!*'

He smiled at her. 'Sure. *I'm* wearing my *pants.*'

'Then you've got the advantage of *me.* Do you usually go bathing in your *pants?*'

'Not usually. But a drop of water can't harm them much anyway, now. Might even do them good.'

She looked at him curiously. 'You aren't from Garwood, are you? At least, if you are, I've never seen you in the village there.'

'No, I'm not from Garwood,' he told her. 'Never been there in my life.'

'Then how on earth did you find this pool?'

'Accidentally. I was on my way to Garwood and thought I'd take a short cut through the woods. I was pretty hot and tired when I reached this swimming hole. So I dove in . . . '

She said: 'I see. Well now dive out and make yourself scarce whilst I get dressed, will you?'

He swam to the side of the pool and climbed onto the bank. He picked up his shirt and went a little way into the woods. There he stretched out and waited. He could hear her humming softly as she donned her clothing again. He gave her five minutes, then went back to the pool.

She was dressed, her wet hair caught with a ribbon and tied back. The white dress was taken tight about the waist with a green belt, the material pulling taut against breasts and thighs. She was sitting on the log where his shirt had lately been, legs crossed, smoking a cigarette.

She smiled at him. 'I waited because I thought I'd better tell you how to get to Garwood. It isn't hard to get lost in this wood — and Garwood's such a tiny place you might miss it altogether if you didn't have any directions.'

'I suppose you live there?' he ventured, dropping down on the grass and stretching his legs out to get the sun's heat on his wet pants.

'All my life — until now. It isn't much of a place — when I tell you that the only pleasure I get is coming here to this pool for a sly swim — well, you'll realize there isn't a whole lot of life in Garwood.'

'I was told it was dead,' he said, nodding. 'But I didn't think it was quite *so* dead.'

'It is. In fact, anyone in their right senses wouldn't *live* there — '

'*You* do.'

'I have to. My home's there.'

'You can always leave . . . '

She smiled enigmatically. 'Are you visiting friends there?'

He sensed she didn't wish to talk about herself and Garwood any more. He said: 'No. Just passing through.'

'Once you've seen the place, I've an idea you'll pass through a lot faster than you intended.'

'Possibly I will. Then again I may not.

The restfulness of a small town's a pleasant thing sometimes.'

'Not when you have it *all* the time,' she mused, plucking a grass blade and twisting it between her fingers. 'It gets more monotonous than you'd ever guess. I know. I was *born* at Garwood.'

He looked at her. 'You don't look — or talk — like a small-town girl. You weren't educated here, were you?'

'I was educated quite close. If you mean have I been to high school, yes I have. But it was a hick high school. I've studied a great deal, though. Books — I wanted to better myself. To get out of Garwood — '

'And you *didn't*?'

'I *bettered* myself — but I didn't get out of the place. I'd rather not talk about it, if you don't mind.' She brought cigarettes from the breast pocket of her dress. 'Will you have one?'

'Thanks.' He took one and lit it with her lighter, then held the lighter for her. She inhaled and drifted blue smoke lazily through her red lips. 'You sound like city. Are you?'

'I've spent a great deal of my time in the city. But I was born small-town like you. *I* wanted to get out — I *did*. Sure, I got out all right . . . '

'Successfully?'

'In what way?'

She threw the grass blade away with a movement that was part gesture. 'Money — fame — power?'

'Money, yes. Not a great deal, but enough. Power and fame I never did want.'

She looked at his worn trousers and his socks, which were a mass of holes. She said, almost challengingly: 'And — *then?*'

'The war. And when I came back, not a great deal to come back to. So — ' He broke off and skimmed a stone out over the surface of the pond. The day had suddenly turned cold. The afternoon was gone and the sun no longer beat down into the clearing. He shivered and began to pull on his shirt and socks.

She appeared not to feel the cold. She pressed him: 'What did you do *then?*'

'Suppose we say that's my business, and keep it that way,' he told her roughly.

She directed a veiled glance at his trousers again. 'Whatever it was, it didn't turn out successfully, did it?'

'However it turned out isn't your business. Or mine either, now. If you just tell yourself I'm a broken-down bum with a sob story it'll be easier not to be so curious. You know what curiosity did to the cat.'

She said: 'I'm no cat.'

Looking at her again, he wasn't so sure. That wild look, that sleekness of body, the green eyes. The sinuous way she moved. Was she deliberately trying to — *tempt* him? But why should a girl like her want to flaunt her sex at a no-good hobo like him? If she wanted, she could have half the men in the state hot on her heels! If she was *that* kind of girl. He realized then that the thing that had been most missing from his life since his return from the army, had been women.

'You seem unusually interested in my murky past.'

She smiled, crossing her legs so that the dress fell back from the smoothness of her knees. 'Why *shouldn't* I be? You aren't bad-looking, in spite of your beard — you're rather young to be a tramp — and anyway, you aren't the type. The clothes you're wearing are well cut, obviously especially for you; they aren't very *badly* worn. So you haven't been on the run for long . . . '

He was on his feet, his face dark. 'What the hell d'you mean by 'on the run'?'

'Don't be so excited. I was just using a term — a phrase. I might just as easily have said 'on the bum' or 'on the tramp'.'

He forced a smile. 'And that's why you're so interested? Because I'm a good-looking hobo who's wearing tailored suits?'

'That, and the fact that you've been in the army — and seem to feel bitter about it. What happened to you? You weren't hurt?'

He laughed. 'Like hell I was; I wound up in England, driving a supply truck, and I stayed there while my buddies got blown to blood and bones in Europe. I can tell you I was *glad* to stay in England at that. I'm no bloody *hero*.'

'Even England had some nasty air

attacks,' she ventured.

He laughed again. 'Not where I was stationed. I never saw a 'plane the whole time. So you needn't feel sorry for *me*.'

She stood up and moved closer to him. She said: 'Perhaps you're bitter about — some woman? Perhaps that's why you're running away?'

'Not on your life. I haven't spoken more than twenty words to any one woman since I got back — excluding you.'

She was very close now; he hadn't noticed, but she must have been edging gradually nearer to him. He remembered the sudden flash of that white body, and his nerves tautened up inside him. He strained to keep complete control of himself. There could be no further doubt; she was deliberately trying to break him down. And another minute —

But she broke the spell herself, by stepping away. She gazed at him, eyelids half lowered again. 'Come on, then. I'll take you to the outskirts of the town. It's getting chilly — the sun's down.'

They walked through the woods in

silence. He was dressed in his full outfit now — pants, socks, shoes, shirt and jacket. She gave him a further cigarette and they smoked as they walked. The way led upwards at right angles to the stream. The wood was still and noiseless except for a few birds trilling their evening notes.

His eyes sought the figure slightly ahead of him — dwelt on bare, sun-tanned legs, lithe and shapely. They travelled upwards to the slenderness of her waist under the green belt and the white dress, then to the entirely feminine set of shoulders and neck and the auburn hair, now drying out in a natural waviness. He regretted that lost moment by the pool . . .

Minutes had passed without either speaking. Then she spoke first, not glancing behind: 'I don't even know your name yet.'

'It's Eddie.'

'Just Eddie? Nothing else?'

'Nothing else.'

'All right, Eddie. Mine's Sylvia — Sylvia Webster.'

He felt that the name wasn't for her at

all — it didn't suit her personality. He wondered what her home life was like, what her folks were like, how many of the village swains she went on dates with . . . and what kind of reputation she'd got for herself in that small village on the mountain.

She continued: 'What do you plan to *do* in Garwood? If you're a hobo you can't be visiting; or can you? And they don't *like* hoboes in Garwood. They're like all small-towners — proud as a hen on a nest of eggs about their dirty little town. They've run many a bum out of town for begging before today.'

'I may try and find a job,' he hazarded, and that drew a deep chuckle from her.

'Every job in the place is earmarked. Practically all the people are descended from about twelve original families. They all act as if the town belongs to them. They make me *sick*,' she spat out viciously. 'The whole damned place makes me sick.'

'Sounds grim,' he said.

'It's gruesome. I hate it. Snooping old busybodies — tattling women — the men having affairs with their neighbors' wives, and those same wives carrying tales about *other* women . . . '

'About *you*?'

She laughed again: 'I'm careful not to give them any tales to carry about *me*.'

'Frightened of your parents?'

She didn't answer that. Instead, she said: 'There's a hotel — well, it's really a tavern, but the fool who owns it likes to call it the Garwood Grand Hotel. You'll get a room there — '

'And what do I pay for it with?'

She was facing him. She said: 'The town is through this belt of trees here. I leave you here — I go the other way. And I don't want to be seen with a stranger, anyhow. The hotel is just on the right at the end of the main street.' She was near to him again. She whispered: 'It's been nice to have met you and talked to you, Eddie. Very nice. I get so sick of seeing the same old faces every day — you wouldn't know. I've really enjoyed myself this afternoon — I hope you haven't been *too* bored.'

'I haven't. Not by any means. If I do

stay in Garwood — can I see you again?'

She shook her head regretfully: 'I'm sorry, no. If you *do* stay — which isn't very likely — but if you do, and we happen to meet, you must act as a complete stranger — you understand?'

He shrugged. 'If that's how you want it. Sure.'

'That's how I want it. There isn't time to explain now. Good luck. And about that hotel room — here, take this.' Her hand found his and he felt paper pressed into it. He didn't refuse; he wasn't that kind of a fool. But he caught her fingers and held them tightly. A flood of desire coursed through him.

'*Sylvia* — ' Then his arms went about her and he pulled her closely to him. Her body seemed to caress him; his lips bore down to hers and found them, slightly parted, moist and soft and clinging. She made no move to embrace him, but there was nothing cold in her kiss.

She pulled free suddenly, and laughed. 'I thought you weren't as cool as you seemed,' she said. 'And this has made the afternoon perfect — almost!'

'Don't go yet — '

'I *have* to go now. If you do stay, maybe we'll be able to go swimming together some time. Maybe. Goodbye, Eddie.'

He stood perfectly still whilst she ran lightly through the trees and vanished from his sight. He fought to calm the thumping of his heart; every nerve in his body was tightened and throbbing. He opened his clenched fist and looked at the notes. They were dollar bills — *twenty* of them! He wondered how a girl living in these parts had got twenty dollars. The answer that suggested itself irritated him. He wanted to think that she had only been like she was with him *because* of him. It annoyed him to imagine her being the same with any other man. He muttered impatiently, thrust the money into his pants pocket, walked towards the belt of trees and went through.

Preoccupied, he stepped into the road — and the car that was rushing along squealed harshly as brakes were thrown on. Eddie never knew what hit him. One minute he was thinking of the girl, and what he would find in the town, having already decided that he *must* stay and see her again. The next, he was struck violently by the car's left fender and whirled sickeningly off the road to collapse at the foot of a tree.

He lay there, still and quiet. There was blood on his hand; one leg was bent abnormally under him. The tree had struck his forehead and opened a long gash in it. The car stopped about five yards farther on, and the door opened. It had been heading towards the town, which was only about forty yards distant. Two loafers who had witnessed the accident came running down the road.

From the car stepped a thin gray-haired man. He seemed neither nervous nor upset. The sign on the car screen explained why. It read: 'Doctor.'

One of the loafers said: 'It was *his* fault, Doc. We saw it.'

The Doctor said: 'That isn't important now.' He completed his examination, rose and said: 'Broken leg — cuts and lacerations. Lift him into my car, will you . . . I'll take him to my place.'

'Sure, Doc. Webster,' said the men.

2

He was in blackness an endless time; occasionally he would become conscious of flashes of excruciating pain, but his mind was dark and he had no idea of the cause of the pain, or in which part of his body it was experienced. Dimly he caught hold of threads from the past: the dusty winding road, the red-faced driver, the halt, the sign which said 'Garwood' . . . and the steep, uphill road . . . the trickling stream.

At that point everything would black out again, and he would start from the beginning, working slowly towards the events leading up to his present state. Slowly his mind cleared; he realized the flashes of pain came from his right leg. He tried to move it, but failed. It seemed heavy and lifeless, as if weighted. He stirred and groaned.

Cool hands soothed his forehead. Something moist was forced between his lips. A soft voice murmured: 'Don't move — you must be quiet.'

Lips touched his brow; he began to remember more of what had gone before. He lay silently, making no effort to open his eyes. Hadn't there been a woman? Yes. A pool? Of course. And a fierce embrace? His memory failed again. He sighed and lost consciousness completely.

When next he came round he was normal. He woke and opened his eyes. He was in a neat bedroom — a lady's bedroom, decorated in a blue and pink colour scheme. The bedclothes on which he lay were perfumed, faintly. There was a bed-lamp, shaded away from him. There was a rosewood wardrobe and dressing table to match the bed on which he lay. There was a chair beside the bed, and a thin man, reading. He spoke hoarsely: 'Hello, there!'

The man downed his book, stood up and came towards him. His gray hair and his features all lent themselves to the illusion of grayness. Yet they were kind features, his eyes good-natured and solicitous.

'So you've finally slept it off?'

Eddie tried to move his leg again and grunted. 'Something's wrong with my right leg — I can't stir it.'

The gray man nodded. 'I'm very much afraid it's broken. Nothing complicated — but it'll keep you in bed for a month or so.'

Eddie said: 'How long have I been out now?'

'About twelve hours. I managed to attend to your leg whilst you were unconscious. How does it feel?'

'It irritates . . . nothing more. Am I still in Garwood?'

'You are. I'm the local doctor. I brought you along to my home. Do you remember what happened?'

'I seem to have a vague recollection of stepping out onto the road leading to Garwood after I'd left the woods — then nothing.'

The doctor nodded. 'Lost consciousness immediately. Well, I'm sorry to have to tell you that it was I who knocked you down. I was returning from a local confinement — you came from the woods so unexpectedly, I didn't have time to swerve or brake properly. The fender threw you against a tree, and your head must have struck the bole.'

Eddie shook his head. 'Can't remember anything of that. Can I have something to drink?'

'Of course. I think you might have a spot of whisky if you feel like it. Do you good.'

'I'll say it will. Thanks.'

The doctor poured from a decanter and handed it to Eddie. He drank it slowly and appreciatively and said: 'Lucky to be alive, eh? Am I still at your home?'

'You are. And you'll have to stay here for some weeks now. If there's anyone you want notifying . . . ?'

'No, nobody. I'm just a bum — a hobo.'

The doctor smiled. 'Then we'll do our best to give you a decent time whilst you're with us. My name's Webster . . . Alexander Webster.' He noticed his patient's puzzled frown. 'What is it?'

'I seem to have heard the name before — *Webster* — '

'It's quite likely. There are a lot of

Websters in the world.'

'I mean in connection with Garwood — '

Webster smiled. 'Don't worry about it until you're a little better. The thing you need now is rest.'

Eddie glanced round. 'I seem to have pushed someone out of this room. I hope I haven't caused anyone any inconvenience?'

Webster said: 'Not at all. Sylvia hasn't any objections to your having her room. In fact, she seemed quite concerned when I brought you here — insisted on you having her room . . .' He hadn't noticed the almost imperceptible start Eddie had given at the name Sylvia. He went on: 'I stayed by the bed to be here when you woke. But if there's nothing more you need, I'll get along to bed . . .'

Eddie said: 'Sure, do that, Doc. You shouldn't have sat up all night, anyway.'

'That's my job. If you want anyone, press that bell-push by your hand. It connects with a bell in my room. I'll come along.'

'I won't want anything, Doc. I'm just

fine. It's a pleasure to get into a real bed again. Thanks for knocking me down, Doc.'

Webster smiled and, leaving the light on, went out. The door closed softly behind him. He left his patient thinking. Sylvia Webster was the girl in the pool! He remembered now. And his heart jumped. So that old boy was her father, was he? Hmm. And she'd insisted on him, Eddie, having the luxury of *her* room!

Eddie stretched his arms and placed them behind his head. He was thinking that things couldn't have worked out finer. If he was laid up in the Doctor's house in this little mountain town, no one was likely to locate him. That was —

He started suddenly. He reached out and thumbed the bell-push.

The doctor was back in a few moments, now dressed in dressing gown and pajamas. He said: 'You want something, after all?'

Eddie nodded. 'Sorry to bring you back, Doctor, but — well, this accident will have to be reported, won't it?'

Webster nodded. 'I haven't made a report yet — been too busy attending to you, as a matter of fact. I'll attend to it in the morning.'

Eddie shook his head. 'Do me a favor . . . don't make any report about it.'

Webster looked puzzled. 'I must. Things like this go on file. But you needn't worry. My report can't do you any harm . . .'

Eddie thought rapidly, then said: 'It can do me more harm than you know, Doc. Listen — I'll tell you about it and trust to your instincts to give you the right angle. You can see what I am: a hobo. But there's more to it than that. I'm wanted by the cops.'

Webster said nothing, but his face creased in a frown.

'Eddie Martin's the name — and I'm wanted for theft.' He was lying, but he was lying convincingly. He pressed on: 'It was a couple of weeks back. I had no money; I was starving. I was in a cheap eating house, and there was no one else besides the guy back of the counter. I was hungry — you ever been so hungry your legs won't seem to hold you up any longer, Doc?'

Webster shook his head. 'I haven't been that unfortunate.'

Eddie put on a bitter smile. 'I hadn't either until about a year ago — then my business went flop and I went flop with it. I had to get out, on the road — I felt so discouraged I didn't care much what I did or what happened to me. So I started hoofing it. That's how I got so damned hungry, Doc. And that's why I knocked out the waiter in the dining bar and scooped the till and a bag full of sandwiches. There wasn't much in the till, only loose change, but it helped me along. When I left, the waiter was starting to come round — he'd had a good look at me before I'd punched him — he'd be able to give a good description of me. So I got out of town as fast as I was able. And here I am — where the cops won't be able to find me. Unless you make out a report — '

'It's unlikely they'll find you if I do,' said Webster. 'They won't necessarily associate you with the tramp who held up a dining bar.'

'But they might. They might be round to ask questions. And if they got me — ' Eddie finished with a shrug, then went on: 'Can't you see how it was with me, Doctor? I didn't *want* to rob the lunch counter. I wasn't brought up for that kind of thing. But when hunger pushes a man to a certain point — something snaps.'

Webster murmured: 'But a *year* . . . surely you could have found *some* kind of work?'

'Do you think I didn't try? Think I lived on nothing for a year? I *did* work. I worked all I could, tried every job they'd take me at. But it wasn't regular — after a week or so the jobs'd fold up, and I'd be on my way again not a cent richer. You ever tried to get work when you don't have any qualifications, Doc.? It's where's your union button, where's your social insurance card, where's this, where's that, where have you worked before, where's your references, where are you staying, have you ever been in jail, and did your grandmother ever have fits, and have you ever participated in a strike, and are your union dues fully paid up! And more than that.'

Webster said: 'I can imagine. So you had to be content with odd jobs — and then, this robbery?'

Eddie nodded: 'That's how it was. I just want a chance to go straight again, to forget what I've done. If they'll give me work I'll do it.'

Webster said: 'Wouldn't it be better to explain to the police and take the sentence you get? It could only be a month or so.'

'It'd finish me,' said Eddie quietly and convincingly. 'Once I'd been in jail it would break me altogether.'

Webster coughed uncomfortably.

'What it boils down to is that my whole future depends on *you*! You can give me another chance — or you can have me tossed in the can and left there to rot.'

Webster smiled. 'I don't think it would be as serious as all that. But — if you feel as you do about it, I suppose the least I can do is to humor you. I was the one who knocked you down, and I owe you something to make it up. But you give me your word you'll go straight if I make no report?'

Eddie said fervently: 'I will, Doc.'

'Then stop worrying. Get some rest, and forget it. Good night . . . or rather, good morning!'

'Thanks, Doc.'

He went out again, closing the door. Eddie relaxed with a triumphant smile. Clearly the middle-aged doctor was an easy man to fool; his heart was big and warm, and he was prepared to take the risk of concealing details of the accident for the sake of helping a lame dog — and *lame dog* was right at that, reflected Eddie, looking at the bulkiness of his leg under the coverlet.

There was a picture on the dressing table. Eddie looked at it several times. It was of the doctor, and read: 'To Sylvia, with my love.'

He didn't sleep again. Somewhere in the house he could hear the sound of a clock striking — five, six, seven, eight. He lay awake, pleasantly comfortable in the featherbed; his leg had settled down to a sort of numb ache now, and he could afford to ignore it. He felt confident the doctor would not now report the accident. He'd swallowed the story he'd been told easily; he hadn't a suspicious nature. He seemed the kind of man who was always willing to believe the best of his fellow men.

Eddie's view was that there were only two classes of men and women existing: crooks and suckers. The suckers were divided into two categories: First-class suckers and second-class suckers. Doctor Webster was one of the first-class variety. Maybe he would be an even bigger sucker yet, Eddie thought, remembering Sylvia. With a daughter like that he was asking for it.

The same clock struck nine. The door opened and a girl dressed as a maid entered. She was a plain girl, with a slight deformity of the hip that shortened one leg. She carried a tray. She said: 'I'm Annie. I'm the maid. Here's your breakfast.'

Eddie grinned. 'I'm Eddie. I'm the patient. I'm ready for it.'

Annie sniffed and set the tray across his knees.

Eddie said: 'How many servants has the Doc got?'

Annie said: 'I have to do it all. I'm about sick of it.' She walked to the door again. 'Your coffee'll be up soon.'

'No cream.'

She sniffed again and limped out. He gazed at the tray. It was neatly set, with an embroidered napkin. It seemed far too neat to be the work of Annie. Sylvia — ?

He ate hungrily, remembering that this was the first meal he'd had for almost thirty-six hours. There were ham and eggs and French-fried, preceded by cereal. There were toast and marmalade. There was half a grapefruit.

The door opened again as he was finishing the meal. Sylvia was dressed in a pale green negligée over a cream night-dress. As she passed the window he could see the outline of her shape through the filmy stuff she wore. Seeing her that way made his blood race even faster than at the pool.

She regarded him coolly. He opened

his lips to speak. She shook her head quickly. Annie shuffled in with a coffee pot.

'Put it down there, Annie.' Annie did so.

'I'll pour for you, Mister . . . ?'

'Martin,' said Eddie. Annie went out again.

Sylvia crossed and closed the door, then drew a chair up and sat by the bed, tilting the pot with delicate white fingers. He said: 'What's the act in aid of?'

She didn't answer his question. She said, evasively: 'Fancy this happening to you. I'd have said you were far too smart to walk out in front of a speeding car.'

'Maybe I was thinking about you,' he returned.

'I was rather hoping you'd forget me. I hoped you'd leave the village without staying . . . '

'Is that why you gave me the money to stay?' he grinned.

She shrugged. 'Perhaps I wanted you to stay in spite of myself. But not in my own home!'

'That isn't so bad,' he said. 'I'll be able

to get to know you much better ... by the way, did you stay alone with me at all last night?'

She set down the coffee pot and said: 'I was with you whilst the doctor got his things. Why?'

'What made you *kiss* me?' he shot out.

'I thought you were unconscious?'

'I was; but I distinctly remember being kissed on the forehead.'

She turned half away. 'You must have dreamed it! It was just your imagination.'

'I guess that was imagination down by the pool, too; and that at the border of the woods ... '

'I guess it was,' she told him calmly.

He forked in his pants pockets hung over the back of a chair near the bed. He produced a roll of bills — twenty dollars. 'Do these look like imagination, too?'

'I don't understand you. Why should they?'

'They shouldn't. You gave them to me!'

'Are you mad? I don't know you from — from Adam!'

Eddie said: 'What is all this secret stuff?'

She looked towards the door. Then, her voice low, she muttered: 'I didn't count on you being thrown into the house in this way. But as you have been, remember this: you're starting from scratch. You've never seen me before — we have nothing other than a purely impersonal interest in each other.'

'That's okay with me. But there's just one thing I need to know before I agree to play . . . *Why?*'

She hesitated. Then: 'I should have told you this before. I happen to be — '

She was cut off short by the sound of the door opening. Doctor Webster stepped in. He said genially: 'Feeling better now? Oh, hello, dear. I see you've met Mister Martin?'

Sylvia said: 'Not formally.'

Webster smiled: 'Then we'll put that right. Mr. Martin — my wife, Sylvia. Sylvia, Mr. Eddie Martin, our patient.'

Eddie's eyes shot to her face. It was expressionless. She said: 'We're glad to have you, Mr. Martin.'

'Thanks.'

Webster chuckled. 'I suppose you're

surprised at an old fogey like myself having a wife as young as Sylvia, eh? But love has nothing to do with age, has it, dear?' He put his arm about her shoulders and squeezed.

She said: 'Of course not, dear. And you aren't old, anyway. You're just at your prime.'

'I'm going along to the village,' Webster said. 'You take good care of our guest.'

'I will,' promised Sylvia. She held up her cheek and he kissed it gently. Eddie's lip twisted cynically.

'Take care of yourself, Alex, dear.'

'I will,' said the doctor, nodding. He went out, and neither spoke until they heard the sound of the car starting up outside.

Then Eddie sneered: 'Wife! So that's the grisly secret out!'

'That's it. What of it?'

'Nothing,' he grunted. 'Except that I thought you'd have had more pride than to marry for what you could get out of a man.'

'What makes you think that was my purpose in marrying him?'

'It's plain enough, isn't it? Why else would you marry him? You don't love him; a blind man could see that.'

Smiling, she toyed with the handle of her coffee cup. At last she said: 'No, I don't love him. I've known him a long time. As a matter of fact, he brought me into the world. When I was a kid I used to think the world of him; and then when I found that I had little hope of getting away from Garwood, and if I stayed I stood in danger of becoming like the other women here, I decided that he ought to — have someone to take care of him.'

'And his money,' supplemented Eddie, ungraciously.

'And his money,' Sylvia agreed. 'So I married him. I made all the running — he was flattered at the idea of a girl as young and pretty as I was wanting him for a husband. He could hardly believe his luck. My God, what a maudlin old fool he was — still is, at times! Fortunately, he has rather a lot of work on his hands; he's the only doctor for some distance, and he's often very tired when he gets home.

That helps to keep him from — worrying me. You see, I have my *own* room.'

'But you'd sell him to any man you took a fancy to!' snapped Eddie. 'Just like that!'

'Why not? I'm young. I have some right to romance, haven't I? It isn't right that I should be tied to a man of fifty-two, is it?'

'You did the tying yourself,' commented Eddie. 'Now you aren't satisfied. The least you can do is give the old fool a decent play. You have his money — what more is there?'

'A lot more. When I married him I was sure I'd be able to persuade him to leave his practice here and start again in a fairly big city. I couldn't. He'd do anything for me — anything but *that*! I had to go on living here; he wouldn't leave these people. He knew them all; couldn't picture them managing without him. He's spent all his life here. He means to stay . . . means to die here.

'He's a clever doctor. He could make a name — be somebody — in the city. But he won't go. Once or twice he's half agreed to do as I ask. And then

44

something's cropped up — Mrs. Carter's baby, or Jake Brown's ulcers, or Linda Norvell's bad leg. That's how it's gone on, ever since we married, five years ago. That's how it will go on — until — '

'He *dies?*'

She was silent. Eddie went on, scornfully: 'Which is what you're waiting for, I take it?'

'What I'm waiting for isn't any of your business.'

'I've met your kind,' Eddie snapped. 'You're angels to look at and devils underneath! When things go wrong the harp you're carrying turns into a trident — and you jab — '

'If we're being symbolic, you don't exactly qualify for a halo yourself, do you?' she said.

Eddie said: 'I've a damn good mind to put him wise to you!'

Her eyes flashed menacingly. 'If you do, I shall go straight to the police, and tell them all I can about you!'

He laughed uneasily. 'You'd just make a fool of yourself.'

'I don't think so. Alex told me the story

you told him. You found it as easy to take him in as I did. Personally, I believe you have some deeper motive than you say for not wanting the police to know where you are. I noticed one or two things when we were at the pool in the woods — '

He eyed her angrily. 'There's nothing about me to hide, I tell you!'

'Let's not try to deceive each other any longer. I've told you what makes me tick. You don't have to tell me anything — but please don't waste your time and mine trying to kid me that you're only afraid of the police because you stole a few dollars; I don't believe it.'

He said: 'All right. You're smart. Mind you aren't too smart one of these days.'

Her smile was irritatingly superior. She said: 'Don't worry, Mr. Martin. I can look after myself. Perhaps far better than you can.'

He finished his coffee and put the cup down. She said: 'Like more?'

'No. I've had enough. Thanks.'

She pushed the tray away and sat on the edge of the bed. She spoke softly: 'What happened in the woods is over and done with. As long as you're in this house there must be no repetition of that incident. It's too risky — '

'How about the risk you took last night? When you kissed me?'

'Let's say I was carried away for a moment. Shall we? Sorry for you.'

'That's a hot one.'

She got up. 'Later, when you are able to walk, we may be able to reach an understanding. There's always the swimming pool where we could meet. Nobody ever goes there — and *then* . . . '

'Meet you?' he sneered. 'You wouldn't get me touching you with a boathook, Mrs. Webster. I think you're a bitch! Your husband may be a prize sucker, but he's a decent enough guy and fond of you. The way you play him for a sap makes me sick!'

Her hand swept forward suddenly. Her eyes blazed. He felt the sting of her palm on his cheek, but his expression didn't change. She hissed: 'If ever you use that obscene word to me again — !'

'Bitch!' he grinned at her.

'You . . . ' She came forward towards

47

him and reached out with her hands for his neck, insane with rage. As she bent, his arms went round her, pulled her down across the bed; his mouth bored down on to hers. Gradually her tautened body relaxed . . .

They lay still, lips to lips.

3

It was minutes before he relaxed his tight grip of her body; before she drew away from him, breathing heavily, with an enigmatic look in her green eyes. She pushed back her disheveled hair with a slender hand and turned away, walking to the window.

He lay still, eyeing her, desire still running madly through his frame.

She said: 'Don't do that again, Mr. Martin. At least — not whilst you're in *this* house!'

'Why worry?' he asked her. 'Your husband's not here.'

'Annie is — '

'You're afraid of Annie seeing something?'

She nodded. 'Yes. Annie doesn't like me. Before I married Alex she used to be his housekeeper. Annie owes a lot to the doctor. She was trapped in a landslide when she was about fifteen — her leg was horribly mangled. They feared she'd lose it. But Alex wouldn't listen to any suggestions of amputation. He took her into his home and cared for her, and through his attention and kindness the leg was saved. Since then, Annie's just stayed on here as housekeeper, until I came, then as maid. She worships the doctor, and she hates me for driving her from his life. If she saw anything — or *heard* anything — she'd go straight to him and tell him.'

Eddie said: 'I get it. She won't hear anything from *me*. I'm going to find it a hard job not touching you, treating you as a mere acquaintance, but I'll try.'

She smiled faintly. 'A few minutes ago, before that regrettable loss of control on your part, you said you considered I was a bitch!'

He helped himself to lukewarm coffee and thought a moment. He said: 'I still think you're a bitch. But perhaps I *like* bitches.'

'If anyone else dared to speak to me like that — I don't know what I'd do. I can't understand why I'm letting *you* get away with it so easily.'

He said: 'Come here!'

She hesitated a moment. Then she walked over to him. He watched every movement. He looked into her eyes and said: 'I'll show you why you let me get away with it . . . '

He reached up and gripped her shoulder. Slowly he drew her towards him again . . . she didn't resist.

Their lips met: his hard and demanding, hers moist and inviting.

The door opened. Sylvia jumped away quickly, startled. Annie entered. Eddie watched Sylvia's eyes suddenly blaze furiously. Her lips, which had recently been so warm and tender, drew into a tight line. She snapped: '*Annie!* What do you *mean* by walking in here without knocking?'

Annie fumbled for words. She muttered: 'I didn't — I'm — I didn't think it mattered with the gentleman being hurt, Mrs. Webster. I'm sorry — '

Between set teeth Sylvia rapped: 'Come here, Annie!'

Annie came, with a scared glance at

51

Eddie. She halted, cringing in front of Sylvia. Sylvia slapped her viciously across the face. 'Knock in future!'

Annie said nothing. Only her eyes told of her hatred for the woman who was her mistress. Sylvia rasped: 'Do you *hear* me?'

'Yes, Mrs. Webster. I'm sorry.'

Eddie said: 'I don't want to butt in, *Mrs. Webster*, but it seems you're being a bit high-handed.'

Annie looked towards him gratefully. Sylvia replied coldly: 'I must ask you to allow me to deal with the servants in my *own* way, Mr. Martin. Guests don't usually interfere with the running of a household.'

'Maybe not. But I'm not the usual type of guest. And this isn't the usual type of household.'

She shot him a warning glance. She said: 'Take away the breakfast things now, Annie.'

Annie loaded the trays and went out. Sylvia turned to Eddie. 'Will you please not interfere again?'

Eddie said: 'It depends. I don't like seeing the underdog get knocked about.

Maybe that's because I'm an underdog myself.'

'There are a lot of things you don't understand, Mr. Martin. And Annie's one of them. She's a slut; you must be able to see that. As long as I'm mistress in this house she'll be roughly treated until she tries to alter herself. Besides, she didn't open that door *accidentally*, then. She was spying. She hoped to see something.'

'How could she know there was anything to see?' he demanded.

'Perhaps she'd been listening, and heard us talking in low voices. If I hadn't jumped away so quickly we'd have been caught . . . that's why I hit her. She *knows* that's why I hit her. And that's why you mustn't give way to any impulses whilst you're here.'

'It's easy to *promise* that,' Eddie told her. 'But it isn't so easy to keep the promise.'

She sneered. 'You were lecturing me about giving Alex a fair deal not very long ago. Do you imagine *you're* giving him a fair deal already, alienating my affections?'

He laughed at her. 'You *haven't* any affections to alienate! But since you ask, no, I don't think I'm being either decent or honorable to your husband. I'd like to be — but as I've told you already, it isn't so easy.'

'Why not?'

'Because of *you*,' he said slowly. 'Don't get the idea I'm in love with you. I'm not. But at the same time — there's something in you that gets at something in me . . . I can't help myself. I'm not making any secret of it — if I don't miss my guess you can feel it, too.'

'What *are* you trying to say, Mr. Martin?'

He shrugged. 'Maybe it's the bad in you that strikes a sympathetic chord with the bad in me. That's about as clearly as I can get it. I hate you for *what* you are, what you aren't ashamed of being. And yet — well, you know what happens when you get close to me and the opportunity's there.'

'You're trying to say that because you think I'm a wicked woman I hold some special appeal for you? You think I'm easy.

That's what stirs you, isn't it?'

He was silent.

She went on: 'You think that given time and place you wouldn't experience any difficulty at all in seducing me, don't you?'

Still he remained silent.

'You wouldn't find it *so* easy, Mr. Martin. I'll admit you're an interesting addition to my life. That I quite enjoy your clumsy love-making — as I've experienced it so far — but I wouldn't permit any risk of a dirty, down-and-out hobo coming between myself and Alex . . . '

'You mean yourself and Alex's money, don't you?'

'Put any construction you wish upon it. But kindly keep your passion under control until I invite it.'

★   ★   ★

It was two long, boring months before Eddie was able to get up and get about with the aid of a pair of rough crutches. They had once belonged to Annie.

Annie had taken a fancy to him, despite

55

Sylvia's belief that Annie felt there was something going on between them. Annie hadn't experienced much kindness in her unfortunate life. Men in the village were apt to eye her rather as if she was some particularly unpleasant reality of life, who should be avoided whenever possible. She was hungry for a little attention and affection. She knew how she must appear to men, with her dragging leg; her plain, almost ugly features; and lank hair. But she lived in eternal hope that someday, somewhere, there might be someone for her.

There never would, of course. But Annie could dream. There wasn't anything to prevent her doing *that*. The way she was ignored, and the very beauty of her mistress, fanned sparks of jealousy and mortification in her breast into roaring flames. It had been that way when Eddie had arrived.

Eddie was something new to Annie. She felt a personal sense of responsibility for his welfare. She took up his meals and his papers, cleaned the room, and ran little errands for him to the village for tobacco or reading matter. In return, Eddie always had a cheerful word for her; his easy personality made her feel that he took a special interest in her. She didn't understand Eddie was as engaging with everyone — that he was built that way.

Sylvia very seldom came to see him during those two months. When she did, she stayed well away from the bed; she seemed to have lost interest in Eddie and his yearnings. He cursed her for that. Often when they were alone in the room, he felt an irrepressible desire to hold her, to press his lips on hers, to draw her yielding body close to his. But she stayed at arm's length, always cool, always smiling and a little superior.

Doctor Webster usually sat and talked with him each evening, after the evening meal, on various matters. He was pleasantly surprised to find that Eddie was a good conversationalist and could talk fluently on almost any topic of general interest; he even knew a little about medicine and surgery. The doctor's heart warmed to him. And the day Eddie took his first uncertain steps with the aid of crutches, Webster said: 'A couple of weeks and you'll be in trim again, Eddie. What's your programme then?'

Eddie frowned. 'I haven't thought about it, Doc. I was getting to believe this was going to go on forever.'

Webster said: 'I've a suggestion, if you care to consider it. How would you like to work for me?'

Eddie said: 'For — you?'

'Yes, Eddie. I can use you. If you care to take a job with me as chauffeur-gardener, I'd be happy to have you. I couldn't afford to pay you a great deal. About twenty dollars a week, live in. But you said if someone'd find you work you'd do it, and I'd like you to stay. I feel a personal responsibility for you.'

Eddie said: 'You don't need a chauffeur-gardener, Doc. Why, your garden's just a flea patch. Ten minutes a week would take care of that.'

Webster said: 'There's another thing. Sometimes I'm out all night at confinements, things like that. If there were a man in the house I'd feel easier in my mind. I don't like leaving Sylvia and

Annie by themselves. If anyone broke in . . . such things do happen. And it's common knowledge they're alone here when I'm on a case.'

Eddie said shortly: 'I rather think you needn't worry about your wife, Doctor.'

'Oh, she's pretty self-sufficient, I know. But it's only an act she puts on. Underneath, she's really reliant on me for almost everything.'

Eddie smiled inwardly. Sylvia must certainly be a good actress to have given him that impression.

Webster continued: 'Besides, I'll enjoy having you around. When I've been working all night and have to drive myself home in the early hours of the morning, it isn't too safe. I'm tired and worn down. If you stay you'll be able to drive me to the patient, drive yourself back here, then call and pick me up again at a pre-arranged time. I enjoy our conversations together, also. It gets a little boring having just a woman to talk to, much as I adore Sylvia. They never see the other side of an argument.'

Eddie said: 'I sure would like to stay,

Doc. But I couldn't take twenty bucks from you for just doing what you've told me.'

Webster said: 'There'd be other duties, of course. I haven't mentioned this before, but Sylvia's always had a hankering for the city life. She'd like to travel to Chicago or New York, or some other big town. Once or twice I've considered falling in with her wishes, but somehow I can't bring myself to leave the hills. Now if you were here, when I'm working all night, or busy in my study, you could run Sylvia along to Midvale. It isn't exactly a fair substitute for New York, but at least it's livelier than Garwood. You could take her in the car, take her dancing, or nightclubbing, or to a cinema. She'd be safe with you.'

'But how about you? Shouldn't you take her?'

Webster shook his head. 'I'm afraid I fall down as a husband on that score. I haven't much taste for the cinema. I'm seeing far grimmer dramas — and comedies — played out every day, in my work. And I never learned how to dance. As regards nightclubs, I can't stand the bands — the racket drives me frantic. But I know Sylvia's been longing to go for some time. That's where you'd step in. I know I could trust her with you.'

Eddie murmured: 'How'd you know that?'

'I'm a good judge of character, my boy. A doctor has to be. I know just the kind of a man you are. Otherwise I would never have agreed to refrain from reporting the accident when it happened.'

Down inside Eddie felt mean and small. He looked at the doctor's honest, amiable face, and felt like a rat. But there was another feeling. A feeling of exultation. *Sylvia*! Thrown right into his hands! He felt pretty certain she wouldn't be quite so stiff and formal once he got working on her.

He said: 'I'm your man, Doctor Webster. And thanks. You don't know what this means to me!'

Webster smiled: 'I think I do.' He went indoors, and Eddie hobbled thoughtfully round to the rear of the house on his crutches. Sylvia was seated in a garden chair. She was dressed in a two-piece sun-suit that molded her figure, and she wore a pair of dark green sunglasses. Her head was thrown back to the sun, and he gazed fascinated at the white hollow where her breasts sloped into the top of her sun-suit.

He said: 'Hello. Taking it easy?'

She didn't look up or open her eyes. 'Hello, Eddie.'

He ditched his crutches and lowered himself cautiously into the grass beside her. He stared up, taking in every curve of her figure. He said: 'Just got through talking to your husband.'

'Alex? What's new with him?'

He laughed softly. 'Seems he wants me to stay here and work for him.' There was a note of triumph in his voice.

She didn't seem very surprised. She said: 'And will you?'

'Naturally. My duties will include taking you to Midvale and dancing and nightclubbing, not to mention guarding you when the old dog's out all night.'

'I know. You'll like *that*, won't you?'

'I will. How about you? Will *you* like it?'

'I ought to. I arranged it.'

He sat up. 'You *what*?'

'I arranged it. I spoke to Alex and told him how useful you'd be, and it was high time I had someone here to look after the house when he was out all night working. He agreed entirely.'

'And — was the idea of me taking you out your idea, too?'

She smiled lazily. 'No. That was Alex's idea. But he always was idiotic. He thinks you're a nice young man. Fancy! You — as my chaperone! Rather amusing, isn't it?'

He murmured: 'He *asks* for it, doesn't he?'

'He does. And it looks as though he might very well get it.' She smiled down at him suddenly. 'Doesn't it?'

Eddie moved his hand until it rested on her knee. 'Sylvia — '

She brushed it aside quickly. 'You *are* impatient, aren't you? I wish you'd be more careful, Eddie.'

'But you've not even seemed to care

whether I was alive or dead since — that first day. You haven't even noticed me!'

'Poor Eddie,' she murmured. 'It's been just as hard for me as for you to keep up the act.'

'Then — you mean — you do feel something for me?'

She nodded. 'I do feel *something*. The same attraction you feel for me . . . The physical side of me accepts what the mental side of me tries to reject.'

Again his hand rested on her knee. She said quietly: 'Take your hand away, Eddie. And take a look at the back kitchen window.'

He obeyed unobtrusively, and caught a sudden flash of Annie's face being withdrawn behind the curtains. He turned back. 'Annie?'

'She watches me all the time. Especially when I'm with you.'

He said, with conviction: 'She wouldn't tell. I'm sure of it. The girl's fond of me. She wouldn't do anything against me.'

Sylvia shook her head. 'Men are fools. You're as big a fool as the rest of them. Can't you understand that a woman may

64

be fond of a man — even love him wildly — and still injure him in some way? Particularly if he doesn't love her? The fact that Annie loves you — oh, yes, she does, Eddie, I can tell — makes it all the more likely that she'll be insane with jealousy when she sees you with me. She hates me already for treating her roughly, and because of my looks. She hates me for being what I am to my husband. Annie isn't as easily fooled as he is. Underneath, she knows quite well why I married him.'

'You treat her rough often, then?' Eddie wanted to know.

Sylvia inclined her auburn head. 'Very often. How do you think it feels to have a maid who hates you?'

Eddie said: 'I can't say she hasn't reason. The way you treat her. But why not get her fired? You can twist Alex round your finger, can't you?'

Sylvia plucked at the waistline of her trunks. 'You don't know Alex. He's hidebound. I have tried once or twice to get him to fire the girl — but he associates her with Garwood and his life here. He was proud of saving her leg — he says if she went, there wouldn't be anything for her in Garwood, or in the world. He says she's a valuable servant, too.'

'But if you insisted?'

'I daren't insist. Alex thinks I'm good and kind . . . ' She caught the half-sneer that passed across Eddie's face and said: '*You* needn't look so smug. He thinks the same of you. But you can see if I insisted she be thrown out, what he'd think of me then.'

Eddie frowned. 'But why does Annie put up with your bullying? She's no stranger to the doctor — why doesn't she complain?'

Sylvia was amusing herself by stretching the elastic at her waist and letting it snap back into position again. 'For the simple reason that she knows very well if she did complain it would mean a showdown. It would mean either she or I would have to go — and she isn't under any delusions as to who it would be. Alex values me far too much. He values my youth and freshness and — as he thinks

— innocence and purity. He wouldn't know what to do if I wasn't here.'

'So you feel safe to take it out of her?' he said. 'By God, Sylvia, you *are* a bitch! The more I see of you the more I dislike your nature.'

She said: 'That word again. I'd rather you didn't use it. And so far as my nature is concerned — well, it isn't that that interests you, is it?'

He said: 'Frankly, I still can't figure out what makes me want you so much; but ever since that first kiss back in the woods there, I've been crazy about you.' He looked down the trail that led to the village. Along the rough cinder road a solitary figure was trudging. He said: 'Who's this?'

Sylvia followed his gaze towards the stockily built man who was on his way up. She said: 'Oh. This is Jeff Rudge, the sheriff in these parts. Must be coming along to see Alex.'

Eddie's eyes narrowed. He muttered: 'Give me a hand up, will you, Sylvia?'

She made no effort to move. She said: 'No need to go. Rudge isn't likely to know you're a desperate character who stole three dollars back in some city miles from here. They don't issue photographs of cheap bums who're wanted in these parts. Not unless they're wanted for something — *serious* — '

He snapped: 'Will you give me a hand up? I don't care to see any strangers right now. They're always too nosy.'

Without standing, she stretched out a languid arm. He caught it and pulled himself upright. The feel of her smooth flesh sent tremors along his spine. Sheriff Rudge was nearer; he released her arm, bent and picked up his crutches. He started hobbling towards the house.

She called after him: 'You certainly don't like company, do you? Not Sheriff Rudge's kind, anyway.' Her tone was mocking, but he paid no heed and went on hobbling until he reached the veranda, vanishing through the door beyond the flyscreen.

Annie was still watching from the kitchen.

Sheriff Rudge halted beside the deck

chair and gazed admiringly at Sylvia. 'Hi, Sylvia. Doin' a mite of sunbathin'?'

'That I am, Sheriff Rudge. How's the trade in wanted men these days?'

He said: 'I don't git ye.'

'Oh, you know. You sheriffs are always wanting someone or other, aren't you? Don't they send you reports and photographs of any criminals who've skipped out of the big towns and might be headed this way?'

Rudge said: 'Oh, sure, Sylvia. But I don't worry any about them. Wouldn't be likely to be any criminals come round these quarters.'

'Of course not. But I'm rather interested in the subject of criminology — '

'What might that be, Sylvia?'

She smiled at him: 'Study of crime and criminals, Mister Rudge. If you don't use those bulletins they send you, I wonder if you'd pass them on to me?'

Rudge stared at her. 'Didn't know you was interested in anythin' o' that nature, Sylvia.'

'I am. Dreadfully. I'm fascinated by the subject. Please, Sheriff. You *will* let me have them, won't you?'

'I'm not supposed to — but — well, if ye promise to keep the deal a secret, I'll oblige ye. But you mustn't say a word to nobody. I'd get into hot water if it was ever found out.'

'It won't be, Sheriff. You can trust me.'

'I know I can, Sylvia. Is Alex in?'

'In his study, I think. Go right ahead, Sheriff.'

Sheriff Rudge nodded. Sylvia said: 'By the way, Sheriff, you aren't wanting anyone right at the moment, are you?'

Rudge chuckled. 'I ain't had to look for no one for years, now. Just came along to see your husband about the chickens he ordered from my farm.'

Sylvia smiled. 'You won't forget the police bulletins, when you come with them, will you, Sheriff?'

'I won't forget.'

He cast a last appreciative glance at her shapely, smooth legs, then she heard his heavy boots tramping over the veranda and the slam of the door as it closed after him.

She relaxed and smiled to herself. She

had an idea those bulletins might be very useful to her.

★   ★   ★

Eddie was lying down on the bed, resting his leg and smoking. There was a tap at the door. He called: 'Come in.'

It was Annie. She said ingratiatingly: 'I got your magazines that you asked for, sir, from the village.'

He smiled at her. 'Thanks, Annie. What would I do without you?'

She simpered: 'Oh, that's all right, sir. I like doin' it for you.'

He fumbled in his pocket and produced what remained of the twenty dollars Sylvia had once given him. He offered her a dollar. 'Keep the change, Annie.'

She rubbed her hands together nervously. She said: 'I don't want the money, sir. I was wondering if maybe you'd take the — the magazines off me as a — a little gift.'

'I can't do that. No reason you should buy me presents, Annie. In fact *I* ought to

71

buy them for *you* — I've had you running about for me a bit too much.'

'Oh, but I want you to take them, sir. And — I got you a carton of the cigarettes you always ask for. I — I couldn't help seeing that the bit of money you had was running low. I hope you don't mind, sir?'

He could see she was desperately anxious for him to take the little gifts. He accepted gravely, then said: 'I don't like accepting gifts from women, but as it's you — I will. And thanks again.'

She said: 'I liked doing it.' She waited.

He said: 'Something I can do for you, Annie? If there is, just name it.'

She said: 'I was just wondering when you'd be leaving us, sir?'

Eddie grinned. 'Well, don't. I won't be leaving you, Annie. The doctor's asked me to stay on as chauffeur-gardener when my leg's good enough again. So you won't be losing me yet.'

Pleasure and misgiving struggled to find a place on Annie's homely features. Misgiving won. 'The *doctor's* asked you?'

'That's it. So as of now you can stop

calling me 'sir' and make it just Eddie. I'll be a servant like you.'

She said: 'Fancy Doctor Webster wanting a chauffeur — why, he don't use his car all that much.'

'I mentioned that. He said there'd be other duties. The garden, for one.'

'Garden!' sniffed Annie. 'More like a rubbish heap if you ask me.'

'I'll soon alter that, my girl. Besides the garden, there'll be you two women to look after when Doc's out all night — and part of the job will be to take Sylvia — Mrs. Webster — into Midvale at night, and give her a chance to see a bit of life.'

Annie's face changed. 'You — you'll take Mrs. Webster into Midvale? Does the doctor know?'

'He suggested it. He claims he's too tired, and doesn't enjoy dancing or nightclubbing anyway. Says I can do the job just as well as he can, and perhaps Sylvia'll settle down a bit more to living here, then.' He looked at her sharply. 'Don't you like the notion, Annie?'

Annie came forward a step and lowered her voice. 'I want you to stay, sir. I like you to be here — I like doing things for you. But — don't have nothing to do with — with that woman! I beg you, sir. I know her. She's — she's bad. She's bad, sir. If — if you let her, she'll get you in trouble. She'll break his heart and yours, too. She couldn't help it — it's her nature. Sometimes when she's been angry with me, it's stood right out on her face that she'd think nothing at all of killing me to get me out of the way. She hates me — no more than I hate her. But — she's wicked, Mr. Martin, believe me. Don't let her make a fool out of you!'

Eddie said: 'Annie, you're making a mistake. Sylvia's all right. You're just persuading yourself into hating her because you were fond of the doctor. But it's all in your imagination. If you try to see things calmly and reasonably, you'll realize that. I know she isn't the sweetest tempered woman you've ever met, by a long stretch. But there isn't anything in her like you think. Now why not snap out of it? I like Mrs. Webster — as a companion. If you try to get the suspicions out of your mind and forget this hatred of her, I feel sure you'll rub along far better with her in future. Why not try it, Annie?'

Annie crossed to the door and opened it. She said: 'You don't believe what you're saying yourself, sir. You know you don't. She's bad, she is . . . and she'll bring you nothing but trouble!'

4

'You're certain you won't need the car, darling?'

Doctor Webster nodded. 'If I do have any calls, I can walk — it isn't likely anyone'll want me tonight.'

'How about Mrs. Wiggins' baby?'

'Not due until the weekend. Besides, if it does happen tonight, it isn't far to her home.'

Sylvia hesitated. 'You know I don't like running off to enjoy myself and leaving you all alone, dear,' she murmured.

Webster patted her shoulder. 'I'll be busy, Sylvia. I want you to have a good time. I know Eddie can take good care of you.'

Eddie, seated at the wheel of the car, grinned. 'Don't worry, Doc. I'll give her a *really* good time.'

'That's the idea, my boy. You needn't hurry back. Sylvia has her own key. Where were you planning on going?'

Sylvia said: 'The Merlin Hotel, Alex. They have dancing and dinner in the Grill.'

He said: 'That's fine. The Merlin's a nice, quiet place. Goodbye, Sylvia.'

She leaned up and kissed him lingeringly. 'I do wish you could come with us, Alex. It won't be half as enjoyable without you.' She got in the car and, with a wave of her hand, she sat back as Eddie started the engine. The car turned out on to the rough road, and the doctor smiled after it and went inside again.

As it vanished towards the village, Annie stared after it with burning eyes from a top window . . .

Eddie eased the car rapidly down the hill, through the small village of Garwood, and out onto the winding road down to the thoroughfare leading into Midvale. The sun was down and the road was wrapped in shadows. It was an uneven road, and the car — which was no elaborate affair — bumped and jolted. As they drew nearer to the cluster of lights ahead, Eddie said: 'Where *is* this Merlin Hotel?'

'We aren't going to the Merlin,' Sylvia replied, busy with mirror and powder puff. 'That was just for Alex's benefit. He'd hardly have taken it very calmly if I'd told him our real destination.'

'Which is?'

'There's a place in a side street off the main road. It's known as the Hole In The Wall. They have some rather interesting floorshows ... and some interesting characters go there. You have to be a member, or be introduced by a member, to get in.'

'Then how do *we* get in?'

'I'm a member. I used to go there with one of the men from the village — that was before I married Alex. It's a long time since I've been and I'd like to see how the place is shaping these days.'

'It may have closed down.'

She laughed. 'Not the Hole In The Wall. It's far too profitable.'

'Maybe the police closed it down if it's like you say.'

'They wouldn't. They get far too big a rake-off in hush money.'

Eddie grunted: 'Why go *there?* Suppose

you're seen and someone reports it to your husband? Why not go to the Merlin? This is the first time you've been to town with me. If anything went wrong this time — '

She snapped: 'You're a *servant*, Eddie. I just want to go there and I don't want any argument.'

'You aren't going. The doc put you in my care — I say we go to the Merlin as planned. What I say goes, servant or not!'

He had never heard a woman's voice sound as cold and dangerous as hers did when she spoke, some minutes later. She said: 'You'd better be careful, Eddie. Don't forget, we know a bit too much about each other to start arguing. If I told Alex that you tried to get fresh with me, he'd throw you out on the spot.'

'*I* could tell him something about *you*, if it came to that.'

'He'd never believe you. He'd think you were being spiteful. He wouldn't take anyone's word above mine. Except, perhaps, Annie's . . . '

Eddie knew he was licked. He muttered a curse.

Sylvia went on: 'I have a particular reason for wanting to go there, you see. Never mind what. Just take the route I tell you.'

He trod on the accelerator and had the satisfaction of hearing her say, 'Ouch' as they jumped suddenly down a sharp dip in the road.

★   ★   ★

The Hole In The Wall was a throwback to Prohibition days. Then, it had flourished as a place where a knowing guy could get his belly full of illicit booze — at a price, and without any danger of interference from the cops.

The city of Midvale had always been corrupt. The police payroll from the crooked element mounted into several hundred thousand dollars per year, for which the police concentrated on troublesome drunks and minor criminals and left the 'big boys' very much alone.

When repeal had come along, bringing with it ruin for some of the beer barons, the Hole In The Wall had faced the dismal prospect of either closing down or operating legally in competition with a dozen or more better appointed clubs. Its owner, Tony Schaparelli, wanted to go on making easy money; but now that a man could buy as much hooch as he wanted at any and every street corner bar, he saw no sense in running the Hole In The Wall along legal lines. He had to have some other draw to bring his regular clients in.

It hadn't taken him long to figure out what that draw would be: a risqué floor show.

'Risqué' was too mild a word. 'Filthy' would be better. So the Hole In The Wall had continued in business, profitably, as a *very* private club; the police had remained on the payroll. Tony Schaparelli had grown sleek and lazy, but had retained his dark good looks and his hard and brilliant personality, which made him undeniably attractive to the majority of the women in his circle.

The man on the door of the club greeted Sylvia with considerable surprise. He said: 'Miss *Corder*! It's been a long time — glad to see you here again . . .

boss'll be glad, too.'

Sylvia smiled, flattered that she was remembered. 'It isn't Miss Corder anymore, Mike. I'm married.'

Mike said: 'So *that's* what happened to you.'

'This is a friend of mine, Eddie Martin. I suppose it's all right for me to take him in?'

'It's okay. Go right ahead.'

They went along the dim passageway to a green baize door at the far end. The passage had paintings and furniture that had been popular in the 1920s. Tony felt that these trappings lent the place an atmosphere. He hadn't changed them since the club had opened.

Behind the door was the club itself. It wasn't large, but the illusion of being back in that period known as the Roaring Twenties was broken only by the sophisticated women in modern gowns. Apart from that, there was nothing to show that the time was 1946 — that the age of bootlegging and spitting guns had been left long in the past. There was a long bar, waited on by a character in shirt sleeves and an apron. The waiters who glided to and fro between the tables were in dark coats over long aprons, and sported handlebar moustaches and bow ties, with high collars. Eddie expected them, at any moment, to burst into song as a quartet. The walls were a mass of gilt and glittering mirrors. The lamps were suspended on high and ornate chandeliers from the ceiling. There was a stage at one end of the room, and when they entered the curtain was down — heavy red plush, with the slogan in gold inscribed across it: THE HOLE IN THE WALL.

They were shown to a table by a corpulent headwaiter, and seated. Eddie didn't care much for the place or the types there. They were mostly drawn from the upper crust of the town, blasé and moneyed specimens of the younger set in search of vicarious pleasures. The women nauseated him. In here they seemed to have thrown off all reserve.

He turned his eyes to the menu and ordered. They had scarcely started when the stage curtain was drawn to reveal a young man at a piano. He was greeted by a burst of applause, and was obviously a firm favorite with the patrons. He advanced mincingly to the edge of the stage and made a bow that was half-curtsy. He spoke in a slightly nasal tone of voice, his pitch high and affected. He said: 'By thpecial requetht I have been athed to thing that old favorite of mine and yourth, 'The Thailor and the Girl from Brooklyn'.' He passed a sensitive hand across his blond, waved hair, and sat down delicately at the piano. He started.

Sylvia enjoyed it; the others in the place seemed to; but Eddie was sickened, hard as he was. It wasn't so much that the actual wordage was bad — though it was bad enough. But mainly it was the actions implied, and the perversity suggested.

He concluded the song and a further round of applause sent him to the piano again, this time to give a special rendering of his own lewd parody to the tune of 'Night and Day'. Eddie was disgusted. But Sylvia almost skinned her hands applauding. He was glad when the act finished. Sylvia looked over at him. 'What did you think of that?'

'Filth and dirt.'

She eyed him curiously. 'You're a fine one to talk that way.'

He shrugged. 'That's how I feel. I'm surprised it has any appeal for you, too. To my mind it's designed for adolescents who want a good tanning. I can perhaps understand it appealing to the feeble intellects of the folks about us, but not to you . . .'

'There's a lot about me you don't understand,' she said, glancing about her.

He said: 'What the devil are you looking for? You've been searching for something — or somebody — since we first got here.'

'I'm looking for Tony Schaparelli — the owner.'

'You know him?'

'I used to know him quite well, in the old days.'

There was another act on the stage now. This one didn't disgust Eddie half as much. In fact, he was interested. It was a dance — of sorts. The woman was nude, and there was a man — it was rather an involved routine. Sylvia looked at him when the act finished. 'I suppose your Puritanical soul revolted then, too?' When he didn't reply, she said: 'You enjoyed that, didn't you? I think you're as strange as I am . . .'

Her eyes wandered again. Eddie followed her gaze — and his body suddenly stiffened; his hands went clammy against the fork he held. Quickly, he averted his gaze from the couple who had just entered.

But he was too late; the man had seen him. He was tall and angular, with fair hair and a small, fair moustache. He came over, dragging the girl with him by the hand. She was a cheap type, a commodity for a pleasurable evening. They stopped by the table and the man slapped Eddie soundly on the shoulders and said: 'By God! If it isn't a damned small world! I never expected to see you again after the army got through with us. How are you, you old goat?'

Eddie turned slowly in his chair. His eyes bored upwards. His face was cold and slightly bewildered. He said: 'Haven't you made a mistake? I've never seen you before.'

The tall man gasped: 'I'm Clayton — Clark Clayton — you remember me — we were in the same company — same place, in England. Stationed at Arrowe Park — in Cheshire. You haven't forgotten, surely?'

Eddie murmured: 'I assure you, you're making a mistake. I haven't been to England, I've never heard of Arrowe Park, and I haven't even been in the army. I was four F. I'm sorry.'

For a moment the tall man seemed nonplussed. He muttered: 'I could have *sworn* — you haven't a twin brother called Eddie Kark, by any chance, have you?'

Eddie shook his head. 'Sorry. My name's Martin — I never heard of an Eddie Kark. I haven't any brothers.'

The girl with the tall man tugged his arm. 'Do let's get a seat, Clarky — people are staring.'

He pulled himself together and said: 'I'm sorry. I could have taken a bet on you being Kark. Excuse me.'

'That's all right . . . no harm done.'

Tugged at by the girl, but with a couple of disbelieving backward glances, the tall man went to a table across the room.

Eddie said: 'Let's get out of here.'

Sylvia smiled strangely. 'So your real name's Eddie Kark, is it? That's interesting. Not that I ever thought your real name was Martin, anyway. But why did you lie to that man?'

Eddie muttered quietly: 'I didn't.'

'Oh, don't lie to me as well. You did. It was written all over your face. He saw it, too, I'm sure. You really *are* frightened of anyone finding out anything about you, aren't you?'

Eddie murmured: 'I said let's go.'

'If you leave now, that fool will be more sure than ever that you're Kark and that something funny's going on. You can't run away like that.'

Eddie sat down again. 'Mebbe you're right.'

'Besides, I haven't seen — Tony — yet.'

'What's the big attraction about him? Why must you see him?'

She said gently: 'I'd like to see him

because we used to be — well, rather fond of each other. He's quite the most fascinating man I ever met. I might have married him if — if he'd been the marrying type. But he isn't. Women are too cheap with him.'

Eddie sneered: 'Were *you* one of the cheap ones?'

She leaned over and patted his cheek mockingly. 'What business of yours is that, Eddie, dear?'

★　★　★

'Tony!'

'Sylvia — now this is what I call a real pleasure! It's been years!'

Eddie said nothing, and glared at the dark-featured man who had come across to the table. The elegant young piano player was back again, trotting out further blue numbers for the delight of his fans, and it was midway through his act that Schaparelli had spotted Sylvia. Now he was standing above her, holding her hand tightly and gazing down at her with admiration on his features. He said:

'You've grown even more lovely, my dear. Tell me, why did you stop coming?'

She said: 'I couldn't help it, Tony. You remember the young idiot who used to bring me?'

'Vaguely.'

'He was one of the first to volunteer for the services. That left me without a chaperone. And without money.'

'But why didn't you let me know?' protested Tony.

She smiled. 'You had so many women — didn't think you'd be interested.'

He expostulated: 'Of course I would! I always thought a great deal of you, my dear. But how have you been all this time? Will you be visiting us regularly now?'

She shook her head. 'I doubt it, Tony. I'm married, you know.'

'Married?' He looked mournful. 'A pity! In fact, a calamity. Who was the lucky man?'

'No one you'd know. He isn't quite — er — from the same circle. He's a doctor — in Garwood.'

'Garwood?' Tony frowned.

Sylvia nodded. 'My home town.'

'Oh, yes . . . I remember now. So you married the local sawbones?' He glanced at Eddie and said: 'That's just an expression, Doctor. You don't mind?'

'Don't be silly, Tony. This isn't my husband. Do you think I'd be talking to you as I am if it was? My husband's a much older man. He's fifty-two — hasn't any use for night life.'

Tony seemed shocked. 'Good Heavens! Why did you want to marry a blasted Methuselah?'

'I had my reasons, dear.'

Tony smiled knowingly. 'I see. And who is our young friend?'

Sylvia looked at Eddie, then said: 'Our chauffeur, Martin.'

Eddie tightened his lips.

'He acts as my chaperone also, in lieu of my husband. You can speak quite freely in front of him.' She made no further effort to introduce Eddie, and Tony made no effort to acknowledge his presence, apparently thinking such riff-raff as chauffeurs beneath his dignity.

He said: 'It really is good to see you again, Sylvia. But we have such a lot to talk over — and we can hardly do it here whilst the show's in progress. Perhaps you'd like to come along to my private rooms for a chat and drink. For old time's sake. What do you say?'

The look in his eyes made Eddie butt in. He snapped: 'She says no.'

Tony raised pained brows. 'Really, Sylvia, is your — er — chauffeur in the habit of answering invitations put to you?'

Eddie said: 'I'm supposed to be here for Sylvia's protection.'

'Then can't you mind your own business until she's in need of protection?' Tony suggested.

'I have; she's in need of protection right now. If she goes along for a *chat*, as you call it, *I* come too.'

Tony glanced at Sylvia. He said: 'In that case . . . '

Sylvia's eyes were blazing. 'Just a moment, Tony. Eddie hasn't *any* say about what I do or where I go. I *accept* your invitation — Eddie can wait here.'

Tony said: 'If he really is your chauffeur, dear, he needs a lesson in servility. He addressed you as Sylvia.

That's hardly the thing. And you call him Eddie, which also strikes a false note. But of course, I know chauffeurs can be very *useful* at times to young and passionate women who happen to be married to old men.'

Eddie got up slowly and quietly. He said: 'Another remark like that out of you and — '

Sylvia hissed: 'Sit down, Eddie! You wouldn't want to start a brawl and attract attention to — yourself, would you?'

Eddie bit his lip and sat down. Sylvia said: 'I'm going along with Tony — Mr. Schaparelli, to his — office. You can wait here, like a good boy. If you don't, I may get mad and *say something* I'd be sorry for, later.'

She rose, leaving her wrap on the chair-back. Eddie sat where he was. He was beaten. She would *always* beat him. She knew too much about him. He watched her walk across the floor towards a curtained recess, behind which lay a section of the club not open to the public. She went quickly, without looking back, with Tony's arm about her slender waist.

Eddie sat where he was, staring blindly at the stage where the effeminate young man was still singing. He didn't hear or see anything. He was gazing blankly in front of him, his mind a cauldron of seething anger. He wanted to follow, grab her by the shoulders, and hurl her back to her seat; he wanted to sink his fist into the dark countenance of the superior Mr. Schaparelli — to have the satisfaction of seeing the thin nose splatter under the impact of his hard knuckles. But he couldn't do either of those things. He could only sit and wait, sipping his drink. He didn't for a moment believe that they were just chatting about old times. That was far too preposterous for him to swallow.

He became aware of someone before him, and he looked up — it was the tall, fair man again. He said, insistently: 'Listen, you *are* Eddie Kark, aren't you? I can understand you not wishing to divulge your real name in front of the lady.' He winked. 'But you needn't be afraid of me spoiling your little game.'

Eddie said: 'What the devil makes you so certain I'm Kark?'

The fair man pointed to a small white scar at the base of Eddie's hairline, just in front of the right ear. He said: 'Remember that scar there? I do. *I did it*. Remember that? When we were fixing the transport wagon and I caught you with the chisel.'

Eddie said: 'I'm not — '

'You needn't worry about the lady. If you gave her a false name that's your business. I won't tell her who you really are. But — you *are* Kark, aren't you?'

Eddie said: 'Yes, I am Kark. Or rather I *was*. Not any longer, though. I'm glad to see you again — but my past life is behind me. I don't want any associations with it. It isn't because of the lady — it's something else. Now do me a favor, Clark. Go away and *forget you ever saw me*.'

Clark said: 'I'm here for a week on business. How about dining some night?'

Eddie said: 'I'm not in town. Just passing through.'

'You seem to know the place pretty well if that's so.'

'*I* don't — the lady with me does. Now blow, Clark! I've left trouble behind me, and I don't want to pick it up again. For

95

the sake of the times we had together back over in England, forget you ever knew me. Eh?'

Clark gripped his hand. 'You needn't worry about me, Eddie. If you're in a jam, I'd like to help — but if you don't want . . . '

'I'm in no jam *now*. I might be if you go blowing it about that you've seen me.'

Clark was curious. 'What kind of jam, Eddie?'

Eddie said: '*Strawberry*.'

Clark grinned. 'Okay. If you don't want to talk you don't have to, and there're no hard feelings. So long.'

He went back to the girl he was with. Eddie breathed a suppressed sigh of relief, and concentrated on his drink. Time passed slowly. The nude dancers came and went again, and the young man with the dainty manner and the disgusting songs tinkled interminably. Eddie sat and drank, and drank some more. He got restless.

He looked at the clock on the far wall. It said eleven-twenty.

The dancers came again, went.

So did the girlish young man.

The waiter came and brought fresh supplies of liquor. Eddie put it where it belonged. He could take his drink and hold it without making a fuss.

The clock said eleven-fifty.

A troupe of girls attired in a few wisps of chiffon came on. When they left the stage they left the chiffon lying on the floor.

The clock said twelve-forty.

Eddie drank some more.

The young man with the lisp sang some more.

The clock said one-ten.

All the performers came on together in a grand finale. The floorshow ended. The curtain fell.

The four-piece band played for dancing, and Eddie sat and eyed the couples drifting lasciviously about the floor under subdued lighting.

The clock said ten minutes to two.

A waiter bustled about with a business-like air, stopping at each table, saying: 'We're closing now, sir — madam.'

He reached the table occupied by Eddie. He said: 'Mr. Martin?'

'I'm Mr. Martin.'

'The lady wishes you to wait here. She says she won't be long now.' He smiled as he said it. He was obviously amused.

Eddie nodded dully. The patrons began to drift out in ones and twos. He sat on. The place emptied out. The waiters rushed round clearing bottles and plates, slamming chairs upside down on table-tops. The barman shot along the counter with a wet cloth. The lights were put off, all except one over the table at which Eddie sat.

The waiter came back, now in coat and hat. He set down a bottle before Eddie. 'Compliments of Mr. Schaparelli, sir.' He went to the door and went out. The rest of the staff followed him. Eddie stayed where he was, alone in the deserted club. He left the bottle before him untouched.

The clock registered two-thirty before there was a further sound. Then it came from the curtain behind which Schaparelli maintained his private 'offices'. A step — and Sylvia came out. She walked unsteadily; her hair was badly disarranged; her dress was crumpled slightly, her lipstick smeared suggestively. She lurched over to Eddie, swaying from side to side. She looked at him and laughed. 'Poor lil' Eddie — wassmarrer, Eddie?'

He said: 'Know what the time is?'

'Does'shn't marrer. Got key — '

'You look one hell of a mess.'

'Had a fine time — ole time's'sh shake. Hie.'

He stood up and put her wrap on. He was blazing inside. The curtain opened again and Schaparelli came out. He was sober. He had a smile on his dark face. He said: 'It's been thoroughly enjoyable chatting over old times, my dear. You must come again — soon.'

Sylvia hiccupped. 'I will . . . trusht me — Eddie'll bring me, won' you, Eddie, darlin'?'

Eddie shook her. 'Pull yourself together, Sylvia. You can't go home this way. Suppose the doc happens to have waited up?'

She giggled weakly. 'You c'n tell'm I only had one li'l drink. He'll believe you. He trushts you.'

'I couldn't tell him anything like that.

He'd see right away you were sotted to the eyebrows. Snap out of it.'

Schaparelli said: 'Maybe the air will cool her off when you get going.'

Eddie said: 'An' this'll cool *you* off!'

His right fist swung up and smashed home in Schaparelli's teeth. Schaparelli hit the floor. He didn't bounce. He lay groaning. Eddie snarled: 'I've been waiting the whole night to do that!'

Sylvia gurgled: 'You shun've done that, Eddie. You — '

He grabbed her arm and almost heaved her towards the passage and the outer door. It was on a chain. He helped her out and left the door swinging. The car was parked at the end of the street on the corner lot. The attendant had gone home. Eddie slid a dollar into the slot of the metal box at the gate and turned out towards Garwood. He drove furiously, over the dips and rises. Halfway there, Sylvia tapped him on the arm: 'Sh — *shtop* the car. I'm gonner be — hic — *shick*!'

5

Sylvia raised a pale face to him. They were by the roadside behind the parked car. Ten minutes had passed whilst he had supported her shaking figure there, his expression showing mingled pity and contempt.

She said shakily: 'Ugh! Seems I — I can't hold my liquor.'

He said: 'The amount you've taken, you wouldn't *want* to hold it. You're doing the best thing. Get it out of your system.'

She bobbed her head over the low fence again, overcome. He waited patiently.

At last she said: 'I — I seem to be — all right now.'

He said: 'Lady, you look like hell! What the devil is Alex going to say when I drag you in looking as if you'd been under the heavy end of a steam roller?'

Sylvia gulped and forked in her handbag, then brought out a mirror. She made a brief inspection and groaned at what she saw. She thought a moment. Then: 'Why need we go home at all? Let's go back to the town and — stay at a hotel.'

'Are you serious? What about your husband?'

She laughed. 'Alex won't mind. We can phone him from Midvale and explain that the car developed some minor trouble which we're having put right at the all-night garage service. He'll understand.'

Eddie grunted: 'If he takes in that story he's a bigger fool than I figured.'

She sneered: 'Everyone isn't like you, Eddie. There has to be a certain amount of trust between married people.'

Eddie smiled unpleasantly. But he said: 'Get in. It'd be better to do as you say than roll you home the way you are now.'

He helped her to the car; she was unsteady on her feet and tripped over the running board, swearing as a sharp burr ripped her stocking. Then she was piled in the back seat and he was climbing behind the wheel. He turned the car and headed back for Midvale. He kept his eyes on the dark, irregular road, but asked over his shoulder: 'Had you any particular hotel in mind?'

'I had. One where they aren't too particular.'

He felt his pulse quickening. He muttered: 'Meaning what?'

'Whatever you want me to mean, Eddie, dear.'

'Where is it? What is it?'

'The Lord Nelson — owned by a man who used to be a British sailor in his day. It isn't very far from the club. I'll direct you.'

The Lord Nelson was along the main street, on a corner. The place was in darkness at that hour, but the doors were open and a dim lamp shed a meager illumination over a porter's desk. Sylvia seemed to know her way around. She indicated that Eddie should park the car in the side street, then they went through to the small reception hall.

There was a seedy clerk at a circular counter. He was dozing, feet propped on a chair before him. There was a bell, which Sylvia rang. The clerk came to life with an exclamation. 'Want rooms?'

Eddie began: 'We want a — '

'Two *singles*,' cut in Sylvia quickly. 'For the night.'

'Singles, eh?' said the clerk, peering at them.

Eddie bit his lip. 'You heard the lady. Two *singles*.'

The clerk said: 'Sure, Mister. Lessee — '

He peered in a dim way at the ledger. He said: 'We got a nice double on the — '

Sylvia snapped: 'Are you deaf? Singles, I said. This man's my brother.'

'Oh, sure. Lessee — we got two on the fourth floor. Pay in advance — three bucks a room. Okay?'

Eddie handed him six dollars. The man rooted two keys from the board behind him. He said: 'You'll have to hoof up. Got no elevator here. Follow me.'

They followed him along the entrance hall and up the stairs. They reached the fourth and he indicated two room doors side by side. 'Sixteen an' eighteen.' He looked at Eddie expectantly. Eddie gave him a quarter. He slid it to roost in his pants pocket, said ' 'Night,' and went.

Sylvia held out her hand for her key. 'I'll take sixteen.'

'I'll open the door for you.'

The door opened and he did things with the light switch. A bed-lamp went on, revealing a plainly furnished combined room with a badly chipped washbowl in one corner and an over-stuffed couch. There was a copy of the Bible on top of the sideboard. Eddie said: 'Fancy having a thing like that in a dump like this.'

Sylvia crossed to the bed and stretched out full length along it. She held her leg up for inspection.

'What d'you think of *that*?'

Eddie said: 'I like it. Listen . . . '

She said: 'I mean the tear in the stocking! I did that getting into the car. They were expensive, too.'

Eddie began: 'Look here — '

Sylvia yawned. 'Like to take off my stockings and shoes, Eddie? I'm too tired to move a muscle.'

He crossed and knelt beside the bed.

She watched with a curious smile. He threw the shoes aside and suddenly clasped her waist tightly. 'Sylvia . . . ' he murmured, bringing his face slowly up to hers. 'We can — '

'No, Eddie. I'm tired. I've had a trying night. I want to rest.'

He stood up suddenly, savagely.

'How long are you going to play hard to get? You *never* had any personal use for me! You just seized on your husband's liking for me to get him to let me take you into town so you could renew old acquaintances without rousing his suspicions. That's it, isn't it?'

She drawled: 'You seem to be satisfied with that explanation.'

He grunted: 'Just what do you think I am? You haven't got that much of a hold over me.'

'It's all right, Eddie. If you like, you can walk right out of that door and out of this town and out of my life.'

His features were taut and angry. He said: 'Blast you, Sylvia . . . I've half a mind . . . '

'Why *don't* you, Eddie?'

He seemed to slump visibly. 'I can't. You know I can't.'

She stood up and patted his cheek. He knocked away her hand with a furious movement.

'Poor Eddie. Honestly, I do think something of you. Remember, I gave you twenty dollars once so that you could stay in Garwood and probably see me again.'

'Then why act like this now?'

She said: 'I'll be frank, Eddie. You're a bum — a hobo. You've no money and no prospect of getting any. You have your uses to me. That's why I persuaded Alex to keep you as a chauffeur. But your uses are limited. If I did encourage your lovemaking, you'd get to a point where you began to think you owned me body and soul. You'd be likely to be jealous even of Alex. And you might give something away — let something slip.'

'And how about that rat at the Hole In The Wall? Mightn't *he* let something slip?'

She shook her head. 'I can trust Schaparelli. And — he may be useful to me in the future. He's very wealthy, you know.'

He said: 'I get it. Your interest in a man rises or falls according to the state of his bank balance.'

'That's about how it is, Eddie.'

'You mean, then, that you haven't any interest in me?'

'I'm very interested in you. But regarded as a prospective lover, you're far too risky. Too hot-headed and possessive. You understand that?'

'I understand I'm wasting my time hanging round.'

She murmured softly: 'Don't give up hope entirely. Not yet.'

He snarled: 'If I had an ounce of will power in me I'd walk out right of here . . . '

'But you haven't.'

'Not where you're concerned. Sylvia — listen . . . '

'No, Eddie. I don't want to listen — not tonight. I want to sleep.'

Somewhat grimly, he snapped: 'Then you're going to be damned unlucky. I'm not leaving this room until we come to some sort of an understanding!'

She raised her brows in surprise. 'Is that the way you really feel?'

'Yes! I'm through being kicked around. I'm either staying here with your consent — or without it!'

'Suppose I screamed?'

He said drily: 'Go ahead. And try explaining to your husband just how I happened to be in your room when the fuss started.'

She beckoned to him. 'I've been wondering how long it was going to take you to get — rough.' She smiled. 'You're ever so much more attractive to me when you act like this. Come here, Eddie.'

He came, and her hand drew him over her, until his lips were close to hers. She murmured: 'Kiss me . . . '

He did. Fire coursed along his veins, and he held her closely until she moved her face slightly. She said: 'I won't keep you on that piece of string any longer. If you wish, you can forget about room eighteen. You can stay here — with me.'

'Sylvia — I've been waiting . . . '

She held him back at arm's length.

'Haven't you overlooked something, though? Alex — he'll wonder if we don't let him know about the car breaking down.'

'Of course. The phone. Is there one in the room?'

They gazed round. She said: 'No. Apparently they don't run to phones here. You'll have to go down to the desk.'

'What should I tell him?'

'What we agreed. Minor fault in the car, under repair. We'll stay in town tonight and be back first thing tomorrow. Alex will swallow that. He's a doctor — he knows it's wisest to swallow medicine. Even if it tastes bad.'

Eddie said: 'Okay, I'll chance it. I'll give him your love.'

'Do that.'

★ ★ ★

Doctor Webster yawned and glanced up from his book at the clock again. His face was creased in a frown.

There was a tap at the door; it opened and Annie came in.

'Yes, Annie?'

110

'Would you be wanting anything more, sir?'

'Not tonight, Annie. You can get along to bed now. I'll wait up for Mrs. Webster.'

Annie shuffled uncomfortably. 'It's turned one now, sir . . . '

He answered rather sharply: 'I know that, Annie.'

'I don't think the mistress will be back, sir.'

Webster said: 'What on earth do you mean, Annie?'

Annie looked confused. 'I don't know, sir. I just don't think she'll be back tonight.'

Webster said: 'I can't understand what you're driving at. Explain yourself?'

Annie mumbled: 'I can't — it's just an intuition.'

'It isn't very like you, Annie. Of course she'll be back. Probably some little trouble with the car has held them up. That's all.'

Annie muttered: 'I'm sorry, sir. I'll go now, if I may.' She went out, and the doctor shrugged and picked up his book again.

He fell into a doze as time passed, from which he was awakened by the sudden jangle of the telephone bell. He blinked, momentarily fuddled as to where he was and why. His heart jumped as the phone shrilled again. The thought that they might have met with an accident came to him. He rose hurriedly and went to the phone.

'Hello? Doctor Webster speaking.'

'Doctor Webster?' The man's voice was thin and strained. 'This is Bishop, Doctor. Could you come at once? My wife thinks she's — '

'Of course — Bishop. How is she? Regular pains?'

'She's having pains about every fifteen minutes, Doctor.'

Webster said: 'I'll be along. Plenty of hot water, Mr. Bishop. This is her first, isn't it?'

'Yes, Doc. I'm worried . . . '

He said consolingly: 'Then don't, man. It happens every second somewhere. Nothing to worry about. You'll be far more help if you keep calm. Got anyone in?'

112

'Her sister's here, Doc. Got three kiddies of her own.'

'Good. Tell her to get everything ready. I'll be along in about half an hour. Haven't got the car and I didn't expect any calls tonight. It's a bit early, isn't it?'

'A week. Doc — she keeps asking for a smoke. Can she have one?'

'Give her a cup of tea instead. And stop worrying. It isn't as if she was ill.'

He hung up. He was a little annoyed. The Bishop baby hadn't been due for more than a week, according to Mrs. Bishop's calculations. He sighed and made for the door to get dressed. Suddenly the phone rang again. He went back and picked it up irritably.

'I'm coming along I told you — '

'This is Eddie, Doc.'

'Oh! Eddie! What the dickens happened to you? I've waited up. Where are you now? I could do with the car.'

Eddie said: 'The car broke down. That's what held us up. I've run it in for repairs.'

'Sylvia . . . ?'

'We had to take rooms at an hotel for

the night. She's gone to bed. She was tired. We had to walk back to town, about six miles.'

Webster bit his lip. The remark Annie had made came racing to the front of his mind. He said: 'Can't you hire a cab?'

'It's pretty late. We didn't think of that.'

'I should have thought Sylvia would have wanted to get back. But if you can't, that's that, I suppose. When will you be home?'

'First thing in the morning, Doc. Sorry this happened.'

'It can't be helped, Eddie. Tell Sylvia it's all right. I may not be in when you do arrive — maternity case. I'll leave a note for Annie to have breakfast ready for you.'

Eddie said: 'Thanks, Doc. That's swell. 'Night.'

'Good night, Eddie.'

He hung up, frowning. Then he shrugged and hurried to get dressed. It would be a cold walk and a fairly awkward one, up higher ground. The Bishops lived in a small farmhouse farther up the hill. He left the house carrying his bag some ten minutes later.

As he tramped on to the rough road he was unaware of the staring eyes that gazed after him until he vanished from sight. And when he was gone Annie sat on, staring from the window . . .

★ ★ ★

Eddie came back along the passage and gripped the handle of sixteen. He turned and pushed. The door did not move.

He looked blankly at it and tried again — same result. He called: 'Sylvia!'

'Is that you, Eddie, darling?' came her voice. 'Did you get hold of Alex?'

'Yes. He was waiting up. Everything's all fixed. This door seems to be stuck. Can you give a shove from your side?'

He heard her chuckle. 'It isn't stuck, dear. It's locked! I locked it.'

'You — *what?*' Eddie nearly yelped. 'I don't get it.'

'That's right, you don't.'

He thumped angrily at the door. 'If you think this a joke — '

'It isn't any joke. I told you I was tired. I am. Good night, Eddie.'

He fumed in helpless rage. He hammered on the panels again. 'Open up, Sylvia. You said . . . '

'I say a lot I don't mean, Eddie.'

He snapped: 'The key to my own room's in there. Open up so I can get it.'

Footsteps crossed the room. A key was slid beneath the door at his feet.

'There you are, dear. Now go along to bed like a good boy.'

He gritted: 'If I could get my hands on you, I'd kill you! You bitch!' He thumped again. A door along the passage opened and an irate head poked out.

'Hey, you! What is this? Quit hammering the hell out of that door and let a guy get some shuteye!'

Eddie grunted: 'Keep your hair on.' To the obstinate door he hissed: 'I'm going — and this time I won't come back, either.'

The irate head raised a cheer. 'That's great. Stick to that.' Then the head was withdrawn indignantly.

Eddie hissed: 'Did you hear me? I'm going!'

Sylvia said: 'I heard you. Goodbye, Eddie, dear.'

With a muttered curse, Eddie stalked along to 18 and let himself in with his key.

★ ★ ★

He was sitting in the hall, waiting, when Sylvia came down the following morning. She looked brighter and far more presentable than she had the previous night. When she saw him, her lips quirked.

'Dear me — Eddie! I thought you were going?'

He muttered: 'I didn't. Can't afford to throw a good job away.'

'Was that the only reason?' she demanded innocently.

He grunted: 'Don't ride me, Sylvia. I'm not in the mood.'

They went out to the car, which was where he had left it. As they got in, he said: 'Exactly what are we going to tell Alex was wrong?'

'Don't tell him anything. He probably won't ask. If he does, say all you knew was the car wouldn't run and we had to

117

have it towed in. He won't examine it — and if he does, he doesn't know a petrol tank from a rumble seat.'

Eddie nodded and geared up. The car swung out on to the main street and along towards Garwood. After the first few miles in a stony silence, Sylvia said: 'You certainly created an awful row last night — or should I say early this morning? Really, Eddie, haven't you *any* shame at all? Wearing your heart on your sleeve that way.'

He snapped: 'You think you're pretty clever, I know. You think you've got me just where you want me — and maybe you're right. But look out — one day you'll outsmart yourself, Mrs. Webster. One day you'll take a tumble — and when that day rolls round, Eddie Martin'll be there to kick the bits around!'

She smiled and relaxed against the upholstery.

★ ★ ★

Annie served them with breakfast. She didn't look at Eddie or Sylvia. Her face conveyed only too plainly what she thought. Her bearing irritated Sylvia, who snapped: 'Why are you looking like a sour grape, Annie? Is anything wrong?'

'Not that I know of.'

'Then try and look a little pleasanter! Where's Doctor Webster?'

'He left a note saying he was seeing to deliver the Bishops' baby, Mrs. Webster. He hasn't got back, up to yet.' She went back to the kitchen, leaving Sylvia staring angrily after her.

Eddie said, 'You play tough with that girl too much. One of these days she'll hit back — hard.'

'She suspects something now, I can tell. But if she ever *dares* breathe her suspicions to Alex, I'll — ' Her eyes gleamed and her fingers tightened about the fork she held. 'I'll kill her!'

He said: 'I believe you would.'

Sylvia broke the tension by returning to her breakfast, and when Annie came to clear away she did not speak to her.

They sat talking on the porch, waiting for the Doctor to come back. Eventually Eddie got up. 'I'm going to shave and wash and change. See you later.'

He went in, leaving her alone. She sat on, tapping a foot in a rhythmic beat on the wooden floor, preoccupied. She was brought back to reality by the sound of a wheezy voice almost at her side. It was the sheriff from Garwood. He carried a cane basket in his arms, inside which six hens fluttered about.

'I brought along the hens, Mrs. Webster. Where'll I put them?'

'Oh, yes, Sheriff. Alex wants them in the cote at the back. You know — the usual place.'

The sheriff grinned. 'The doc's mortal fond of chicken, eh? You'll be livin' on it for the next few weeks.'

'I expect we will, Sheriff.' She went round with him and watched the hens placed squawking into the pen. Then she walked back to the road by his side.

He said: 'When he gets round to wantin' some more, he can have them. I got plenty of stock this summer.'

'He'll let you know, Sheriff. Oh, by the way — ' she tried to sound casual. 'Did you bring me any of those wanted circulars?'

He said: 'Cracky, I dern near forgot! Must be gettin' hazy in my old age. There's some oldish ones I brought along, Sylvia. Can't afford to part with this month's yet.'

He forked a wad of much-thumbed papers from his pocket and gave them to her. She took them eagerly. 'Thank you, Sheriff.'

'By the way, I see you got a young man staying with you recent. Relative?'

'No, Sheriff. Just a servant.'

'Been here long?'

'A couple of months now.'

'Since about the time your husband knocked down that young feller near the village?'

She replied calmly, though her heart was thumping. 'Why, yes, as a matter of fact it's the same man.'

He nodded. 'I been expectin' your husband to report that accident, Sylvia. How come he didn't? The two boys who helped the doc pile him in the car after it had happened seemed to think he was pretty badly knocked about. I only got to know from them this week.'

'He only *looked* bad. It wasn't anything really. Just a bump on the head. Wasn't worth reporting even.'

'Well, long as he's all right now. Working for your husband, is he?'

'As chauffeur. He was down-and-out and Alex wanted to help him get on his feet again.'

The sheriff nodded. 'Mebbe I'll come along and have a chat with him some time. Ought to keep an eye on strangers to the place. That's part o' my job. Good day, Mrs. Webster.'

'Good day, Sheriff.'

She watched him go, then returned to the chair on the porch. She looked about her carefully before she laid the wanted circulars on her knee, and began to glance through them eagerly. She came to the third, dated two months previously. She opened it — then stared, fascinated. She stared for a long time, reading and re-reading the lines of type beneath the blurred photograph. Then slowly she folded the circular up and slipped it down the neck of her dress. The others she screwed into a ball, placed beside her, and set a match to. She waited until they were nothing more than charred ashes, and ground them into the woodwork with her foot.

The smile on her face was one of triumph. She went into the house.

And Annie, who had been watching from the front window, which she had been cleaning, went hurriedly back to the kitchen with much to think about.

* * *

Doctor Webster laid his bag down wearily and sank into his large armchair. Sylvia came and sat on the arm of it and ran a soft and soothing hand over his graying hair. 'You've been a long time, dear.'

He nodded. 'She sent for me far too soon. Got frightened. But it's a fine baby. Eight pounds. She can be proud of it.'

Sylvia said: 'You're proud of it, too, aren't you? You're proud of all the babies round here that you deliver.'

He smiled. 'I take an interest in the

families, of course. I started my practice here, meaning to move once I'd saved a little money; and then I suddenly found I didn't want to leave. The folks here wanted me — and I liked them. They're so genuine about everything.'

'But they don't always pay, do they?'

'They can't, always. They have hard times, like the rest of us. But if they can't pay in cash, they pay in kind.'

She pouted: 'Why don't you leave, darling? We could go to some city. You could retire. You've enough saved.'

'I'd go to pieces if I stopped working.' He smiled. 'And somehow I'd feel guilty if I left these people. There isn't any guarantee that another doctor would take over the practice. I imagine they'd all fight shy of it.'

'But you aren't getting any younger, Alex. You'll have to retire sometime. Why not now?'

'We've been over all that, Sylvia,' he said reproachfully. 'I know it's hard on you being stuck up here — that's why I agreed to hire Eddie, mainly to take you to town now and then.'

'But that isn't the same as living in town,' she told him petulantly.

He said: 'Let's forget it for now, eh, dear? I'm rather hungry. I hope Annie has something ready.'

As she watched him walk towards the kitchen, her gaze was vindictive.

6

'Money isn't very important in the scheme of things,' said Webster, smiling. 'When you're a little older, Eddie — and you, too, Sylvia — you'll find that out.'

They were seated in what the doctor liked to call his library — actually, it was the small front room of the frame house, and contained no more than about fifty medical works on a squat shelf at the window recess. The conversation had drifted on to easy ways of making money, the way conversations do. Webster had listened, smilingly, to a dozen harebrained schemes that Eddie had assured him would come off if he only had capital enough to start them. Then he had propounded his own views.

Sylvia said chidingly: 'That's only *your* conviction, Alex. I admit money doesn't stand for a lot up here — but elsewhere money's the most powerful asset a man can have. For instance, in New York it wields far more power than crowned heads.'

Webster said: 'But it doesn't bring happiness. Folks up here are happier in their own small-town way than New Yorkers can ever be.'

Eddie said: 'I don't know so much. Give me a hundred thousand dollars and I guarantee you I'd be happier than any of these hicks hereabouts ever were or will be.'

The telephone jangled, and Webster said: 'I'll get it. It may be the Hoffenheim family. Two of the kids are down with measles. I told them to call me if they ran any higher temperatures.' He picked the phone up and said: 'Yes — yes, the Webster residence. Who — ? Just a minute.' He turned round. 'For you, Sylvia.'

'Me? Who'd be calling me?' She took the phone from him. 'This is Mrs. Webster . . . who? Oh — !' Eddie thought he caught a startled look in her eyes for a moment. Then it was gone. She said: 'Oh, yes. Come down to Midvale? Tonight? Well, I don't know . . . maybe. Yes, I'd like to have a talk with you. I'll see . . . about eight?' She held the telephone covered and turned to Alex. 'Alex, it's an old friend of mine. A girl who used to live in the village. She wants to see me — she's staying in Midvale for a few weeks and wants to know if I can visit her tonight. Is it all right, dear?'

He said: 'A *girl* friend? That sounded like a man's voice to me.'

'Oh, of course, that was just her husband getting through for her. It *will* be all right, won't it?'

Webster said: 'All right as far as I'm concerned, Sylvia. Eddie'll run you there. Won't you, Eddie?'

Eddie said: 'That's what I'm paid for.'

Sylvia spoke into the mouthpiece again. 'Yes, I'll be along, dear. Eight? Right. Goodbye.' She hung up and returned to her seat.

Webster said: 'I think I'd like to come along, too, on second thoughts. I need some relaxation at the moment. You wouldn't mind, dear?'

Sylvia said: 'Of — of course not. But — how about the Hoffenheims? Suppose something goes wrong?'

Webster said: 'Oh! I was forgetting the Hoffenheims. I'm afraid I won't be able to go after all.'

Sylvia smiled. 'You'd only be bored to tears anyway, darling. Milly Blake isn't exactly intellectual company. She seems to have only one topic of conversation — Milly Blake. I know you wouldn't like her.'

Eddie said: 'It doesn't sound like a jolly evening for me, either.'

'Oh, you can stand it, Eddie. It won't hurt you. I'm not looking forward to it myself, but we used to be rather good friends before I married Alex — and I feel I ought to make an effort to see her. It's better than having her push herself on us up here, anyhow.'

Webster said: 'I expect this means you'll want the car?'

'We can hardly walk, Alex.'

'You could walk as far as the road and take the cross-country coach. There's one every half hour, and I may need the car tonight.'

Eddie cut in: 'Sure we can take the

coach. Sylvia wouldn't want to be responsible for delaying you if you did get a call to go to those sick kids, would you, Sylvia?'

Sylvia said: 'Why — no, of course I wouldn't.'

Webster said: 'You don't mind, do you, dear? I know you hate motor coaches, but with the Hoffenheim kids being sick — '

She kissed him gently on the forehead. 'Of course not.'

He yawned and got up. 'I think I'll turn in for a nap. Didn't get a wink last night, and I may be up all night tonight, too. I'll see you before you leave.' He left the room.

They listened to his footsteps going upstairs, then Eddie said: 'Suppose you go see your girl friend alone — I'll take in a movie and pick you up after you've done your jabbering.'

Sylvia stared at him. 'That wasn't any *girl* friend . . . That was Schaparelli!'

Eddie snapped: 'Then be damned to it! If you think I'm going to sit like a blasted poltroon again for another three or four hours while you and he — '

'You've got it wrong. It isn't that. Yes, he wants to see me tonight, but he doesn't want to chat about old times *this* time.'

'Maybe this time he wants to chat about new times.'

'He wants to chat all right,' she said. 'He wants to chat about how much I can pay him.'

Eddie sat up. 'For what? His favors?'

'For not informing my husband of our little party in his office last night.'

Eddie sneered: 'You mean blackmail? So that's your fine friend, Mr. Schaparelli! That's the gent who'll keep his trap shut! A dirty blackmailer!'

Sylvia said: 'Don't rub it in. I didn't have any idea he was like that. Even now I can't believe he isn't joking.'

'But you daren't risk *not* going. You know what a rat he is and you're afraid he means what he says.'

'I am.'

Eddie said: 'Why worry? He can't prove anything. It's his word against ours.'

'It isn't only his word. He has photographs. It seems he has a hidden camera especially for taking them.'

Eddie exploded: 'The louse! I wonder how many women he's taking money from through that device!'

'Judging by the women I know him to have had affairs with, it'll be plenty. And now he knows I'm married, he's taken the first opportunity of adding me to their ranks.'

'I've no sympathy, anyway. You got yourself into it — now start wriggling. I told you you'd outsmart yourself one day. This is it, sooner than I thought!'

She snapped: 'You're in it as much as I am! If Alex finds out just how little you are to be trusted after all — he'll kick you out so fast the seat of your pants'll scorch!'

Eddie scoffed: 'I shouldn't worry about that. It's nothing compared to what you've got coming to you.'

She suddenly changed tactics. She held his arm tightly. 'You *have* to help me out of this, Eddie! You have to! I can't handle a thing like this alone. Come with me to see what he wants!'

'Not a chance!'

Her eyes met his; she moved closer. 'Eddie, if you'll help me out of this scrape — I promise I won't kick you round any more. I mean it, Eddie.'

He sneered. 'Like you meant it when you locked me out of your room last night?'

'I swear it this time, Eddie. I'll be the way you want me to be with you. I'll do anything. Just help me out of this jam, Eddie, please. You couldn't run out on me *now*!'

He began to soften. 'Suppose I give you this chance and do help you. How the devil do I do it? I've got no money to pay him.'

'We'll think of something. Just come along with me. I can't face him alone. Will you, Eddie?'

Eddie thought for a moment. 'I don't like that character, anyhow. Okay, I'll come. Maybe we can think of something.'

Sylvia suddenly hissed: 'Shhh!'

He stopped talking. From the open doorway Annie said: 'Is there anything you were wanting in the village, Mrs. Webster? I'm going down there now.'

Sylvia said: 'Nothing, Annie. Nothing.'

Annie went. Sylvia went to the window and watched her walking down the trail. Eddie said: 'How long had she been there?'

'I don't know. I don't know if she heard anything. I hate that girl — always watching, listening, snooping about. One of these days . . . '

Eddie said: 'Ten to one she heard nothing and isn't even spying on you. It's probably a fixation you've got.'

'It isn't a fixation. She's trying to catch me out — and she will, one of these days.'

Eddie said: 'I'd hate to have your conscience. Guilty as hell.'

Sylvia snapped: 'Your own isn't too easy, is it?'

He came swiftly to his feet. 'You keep making remarks like that! Just what do you mean?'

She changed suddenly and said: 'Nothing. Just talk. Don't let's row now, Eddie. Just when we're beginning to understand each other.'

Eddie grunted: 'I'll *never* understand you!'

Sylvia eased her shoe off and groaned. 'What a trek. At least Alex might have run us down in the car as far as the road here.'

'How could he? He might have had a call at any minute.'

Sylvia snorted: 'Measles isn't that serious. I do believe he didn't *want* me to have the car.'

'Can you blame him after the time he must have had last night hoofing it to that confinement?'

She glanced at her wristwatch. 'Coach isn't due for almost ten minutes.' She sat on the fence and held up her unshod foot. 'Tickle my foot, Eddie.'

Eddie growled: 'Tickle your *own* foot. Mine feel just as sore as yours do. Somebody ought to do something about smoothing that road down.'

Sylvia pouted and started rubbing her silk-clad foot. The sun was down and the night was getting chilly. Eddie said: 'I hope we don't have to stand on this bus.'

'We won't have to. People who don't

live in Midvale or surrounding districts have the sense to stay away as a rule. Midvale hasn't anything to offer to out-of-towners.' She pulled on the shoe again. 'Have you thought of any way of putting Schaparelli off?'

'Have you?'

She said: 'Perhaps I have — if all else fails.'

He glanced at her sharply, but said nothing.

There was a distant rumble. Sylvia said: 'That sounds like the bus now. Yes — there it is, over the rise.'

As the coach drew level she stepped forward and waved. The driver executed a smart piece of braking and the coach squealed to a stop almost within its own length. The driver pulled his control lever and the sliding door shot open. They climbed up the high step and the door shut behind them.

'Where to?'

'Midvale.'

He gave them a ticket and change from the rack in front of him. Then he released the brakes and the bus rolled on its way.

As Sylvia had predicted, the coach was almost empty. There was an old lady at the back carrying a large basket of flowers. In the front seat were a couple of kids, a boy and girl. By the cut of the boy's jacket and the swing skirt the girl wore, Eddie judged they were going along to some groovy dance in Midvale. He looked at them a little wistfully.

The driver was a conversationalist. As they passed a derelict farmhouse some way out of town, he said: 'I remember when that place was struck by lightnin'. Some blast, that was. It ain't fit for no one, now. An' no one ever went to the trouble to rebuild it. Nope. The folks that were in there were all killed. Place burned right down, well alight before they were able to wake and scream out. I stopped the coach about here to lend a hand, but no one could have saved them. They had bars up over the windows and that stopped them escapin'. Boy, did they scream! You never heard a thing like it.'

Eddie shuddered. He liked to think he was tough, but talk like that conjured up unsettling mental pictures. The driver prattled on: 'Reckon this route's losin' money for the company. No one ever wants to go to Midvale these days. I remember once when it used to be quite a joint. Bus was full every night. But that was before they repealed prohibition. A man could get his gutful of bootleg in Midvale then. Now he only has to go as far as the corner saloon.'

No one was listening to him. But he went on talking. Sylvia was staring from the window beside her. Eddie was wondering just what she had meant by that remark about having thought of some way to deal with Schaparelli, if all else failed.

The two kids were gazing into each other's eyes. The old lady was dozing with the jolting motion of the coach. They rumbled through the outskirts of Midvale, and braked at the end of the main street.

'Midvale.'

Sylvia and Eddie got out, and so did the two kids. The bus rattled on.

★　★　★

Schaparelli sat at a reserved table in his club in a secluded corner. Occasionally he glanced at the green-figured clock over the door. Now it said eight-oh-two. His visitors were only two minutes late so far. But Schaparelli felt that their business was of such paramount importance that they should have arrived dead on time, if not slightly before. The lateness argued that Sylvia Webster was not as perturbed as she should have been. Schaparelli smiled and told himself he'd soon alter that when he'd had a word or two with her. He wondered if she'd bring along the man she called her 'chauffeur'. If she did, Schaparelli had a nice little surprise for him. People couldn't go busting men like Schaparelli on their aristocratic noses and get away with it. He looked at the clock again. Eight-oh-five.

The entrance door opened up and Sylvia came in, followed by Eddie. They hadn't checked their coats. They stared round, and the headwaiter hurried across in answer to Schaparelli's nod.

'Mrs. Webster?'

'Mr. Schaparelli expects us.'

'Yes, Madam. Will you come along with me?' As arranged, he took them straight to Schaparelli's private apartments attached to the club. He indicated chairs. 'Mr. Schaparelli will be here in a moment, Madam.' He went back into the club and nodded to Schaparelli. Schaparelli, in turn, caught the eyes of two 'gentlemen' in evening dress seated at a table nearby. They rose and came over casually.

'In about ten minutes,' he said. 'But stay close in case anything goes wrong. The man with her may try to be awkward.'

They nodded. One said: 'We give you ten minutes, then bust in and carry out the arrangements. Is that right, boss?'

'Yes. You know just what to do. If you hear anything that sounds like trouble before the ten minutes is up, come anyway.'

Schaparelli got up and walked elegantly across to his private rooms, exchanging smiles with one or two ladies he knew. The stage show was on the point of starting. He passed close to the leader of the small band outfit and murmured: 'Keep it good and loud, Turner.'

'Rely on it.'

Then he went through and into his rooms. Sylvia was seated on a low divan in front of a cheerful fire; she looked composed now. Eddie seemed more ill at ease. He was standing beside the divan with his hands at his sides.

Schaparelli said: 'I'm so glad you could come.'

Sylvia snapped: 'If that phone call was a joke, I don't like it.'

Schaparelli murmured: 'Joke? It was no joke, my dear Sylvia. Far from it — Look.' He pointed to the far wall. There was a gilt mirror there. He said: 'You've heard of two-way mirrors? To you, or anyone in this room, it's a mirror and nothing more. But behind, looking through, a person on the other side has a perfectly clear view of this room. A camera can take an excellent shot from there — you'll notice that the lights are neatly arranged, and exceptionally strong. Didn't you wonder at that? Surely, if I were only interested in romance, I'd have *dim* lighting?'

Eddie spoke for the first time. 'I classed you as a rat the first time I saw you.'

Schaparelli said calmly: 'That is of no interest to me. If women are foolish enough to enter into illicit relationships with me, they deserve all they get. Money is a very useful commodity — at least, I find it so. You would have been well advised to stick to — *chauffeurs*, my dear Sylvia.'

Eddie's fists tightened but he made no move.

Schaparelli said: 'If you still doubt me, perhaps you'd better have a look at these.' He took a small envelope from his pocket and gave it to Sylvia, who opened it and extracted three small photographs. Her lips came together in a thin line.

Schaparelli said: 'I wonder how your middle-aged doctor would react to three enlargements of those on his breakfast table?'

Eddie took them from Sylvia and looked at them. He slid them back in the envelope; he couldn't refrain from giving Sylvia a contemptuous look.

'Notice how your own chauffeur looks

at you, my dear?' said Schaparelli mockingly. 'How much more so your own husband?'

Eddie turned and threw the offending photographs into the fire, watching them leap into flame. Schaparelli sighed: 'How easy it would be if that were all you needed to do to destroy them. But naturally I have the negatives.'

Sylvia said: 'You make me sick. All right, how much?'

Schaparelli placed his fingers together thoughtfully. He said: 'I remember you saying last night that your husband had been a careful man. That he had a great deal of money saved. I think the sum you mentioned was — fifty thousand dollars, was it not? About that figure.'

'I was drunk last night. I didn't know what I was saying. I was — boasting, trying to make my marriage seem important.'

'Nevertheless I believe you,' said Schaparelli. 'I will not name too high a figure. Suppose we say — twenty thousand?'

Sylvia laughed harshly. 'You must be

crazy. Alex wouldn't give me *twenty* dollars unless he knew what purpose I wanted it for. How on earth could I get twenty thousand from him?'

'I am only interested in acquiring the money. How you obtain it will not be of the least interest to me. Possibly your — chauffeur — can help you.'

Sylvia said: 'I can perhaps raise about five hundred dollars. If you'll take that — I'll promise to pass on any other sum I can get hold of in the future.'

Schaparelli said: 'I'm not disposing of these very excellent photographs on hire-purchase terms. If I wished, I could have reproductions printed and sell them to a gentleman I know for general distribution in the town at one dollar a print. I fancy they'd sell like hotdogs on a January morning.'

'You — you wouldn't — '

'Why not? You will notice that I took care to have my own face looking away from the camera. You are the only one who could be properly identified.'

Sylvia said: 'Then — you won't take — anything less?'

'Twenty thousand. I'll give you until tomorrow night to find the first five. If you fail — '

'That's impossible. Even for five thousand I'd have to handle Alex carefully. When it comes to money, he's on the tight-fisted side. If you'll give me, say — a month, I'll do what I can, but — '

'Tomorrow night,' said Schaparelli.

Eddie said: 'And if she doesn't get the money?'

'Then her husband gets the prints — enlarged to six by eight. They should prove quite an attractive little set. Although I can hardly picture him having them framed and hung in his reception room.'

Sylvia stood up. 'I'll *try*.'

'Do, my dear Mrs. Webster. And for your own sake, try hard.'

Eddie grunted: 'Come on. Let's get out of here. The place has a funny smell.'

Schaparelli raised a detaining hand. 'Don't hurry away. There are two gentlemen outside who are rather anxious to make your acquaintance.' He walked to the door and opened it. The blare of the band welled into the room. 'You can come in now, gentlemen.'

Two large and capable 'gentlemen' in evening suits came into the room. One jerked a thumb at Eddie. 'This the mug?'

'He is. Mug enough to walk back here after having the temerity to strike me.'

Eddie started to move forward. 'I'm warning you, Schaparelli . . . '

'That's nice of you, Mr. Martin. Wait a minute, boys — remove the lady first. After all, this won't be any sight for the fairer sex.'

Sylvia was visibly perturbed. 'What — what are you going to do to Eddie? You aren't going to — '

'Do I look a fool?' sneered Schaparelli. 'Of course I'm not. But he does need a lesson. He mustn't go about hitting people on the nose.' He broke off with a yelp. Eddie was quite close to him. The two 'gentlemen', as Schaparelli had termed them, were nearer the door. And Eddie had taken a pace forward and neatly placed another punch on Schaparelli's aristocratic nostrils.

The next second he was held in the vice-like arms of the two 'gentlemen'. Schaparelli, fuming, his nose streaming blood, lost his control. He said: 'I'll attend to him myself.' He gripped Sylvia by the shoulders, whirled her protestingly over to the door, and almost hurled her out. He shut the door and slipped the bolt home.

She bumped into the opposite wall and stood there weakly, holding on to her control. She was really afraid of what they might do to Eddie. She hadn't thought she cared that much. There was a hoarse cry from inside the room. Her fingers went tighter about her bag. Minutes passed; the cry from the room was not repeated. Then the door opened. Schaparelli said: 'Come in.'

She went in, fearful of what she might see. Eddie had gone. Only the two 'gentlemen' were in evidence. But there was an ominous smear of blood on the floor.

Schaparelli said: 'We showed your friend out by the back entrance. He was hardly presentable enough to go out through the club. Monaghan, here, will

escort you to the back door. You'll
probably find Mister Martin in the entry.
You'll doubtless be able to console him.
And I warn you for the last time — that
money must be in my hands by tomorrow
night, or I shall make a special point of
having those prints sent to your doting
husband. And by the way — don't bring
Mr. Martin here again. I've taken a dislike
to his face, I fear, and the treatment we've
just meted out to him hasn't improved it
at all.'

'What have you done to him?'

Schaparelli smiled: 'I expect he'll tell
you that fast enough himself. He
wouldn't be so indiscreet as to report the
affair, however, in view of the facts
concerning yourself which would be sure
to see the unpleasant light of publicity if
any court action arose.'

One of the large 'gentlemen' took her
arm and hustled her towards a curtained
alcove at the rear of the room.

Schaparelli said: 'Tomorrow!'

Then she was being pushed roughly
along a narrow whitewashed passage,
through a wooden door, and out into the

yard of the club, where empty bottles and cases and barrels were scattered in profusion. Then across the yard to the yard door, and through it. The 'gentleman' known as Monaghan grinned. 'Good night, lady. An' pleasant dreams! Haw, haw!' Then the door was slammed and a bolt was driven home.

Sylvia stared round the dark, deserted entry, screwing up her eyes in an effort to combat the darkness. There was a shadow against the opposite wall, half doubled up, holding the wall for support. A low groan came from that direction.

'Eddie!'

He muttered something, his voice hoarse and blubbery.

'Oh, Eddie! What did he do to you?'

She ran over and took his arm. He mumbled indistinctly. 'He got his two uglies to hold me still — while he put a pair of iron knuckles on and dusted me in the teeth with them! Ugh!'

She choked: 'The swine!'

They started moving, Eddie hanging on to her arm. As yet he wasn't in very good shape. He was still half dazed from the terrific blow he had taken from Schaparelli's knuckle-dusters. But he barked grimly, as they gained the end of the entry: 'I'll get him for this — he can't do that to me! Not to me!'

They came under the light of a lamp, and what Sylvia saw made even her feel sick to the stomach. The dusters had landed squarely in Eddie's mouth. His lips were split and smashed; his teeth had been broken. The lower half of his face was covered in blood. His nose was a red stream. His cheeks were already showing purple bruises.

'Eddie — !'

'I'd better find a gent's toilet and clean myself up,' he mumbled thickly. 'Can't hop round this way. I suppose I'm fairly messed up?'

'You need a doctor.'

'I can wait until we get back for that. Just let me get washed up for now.'

They began to walk slowly down the main street. She said: 'I've got it in for Schaparelli more than ever now. Get cleaned up and then we can think it out . . . He deserves to die!'

7

Eddie got cleaned up. His injuries, which had seemed serious, now proved to amount to nothing more than a couple of split lips, a slightly squashed nose, and bruised cheeks. Behind the split lips, two of his teeth had sustained the full impact of the knuckle-dusters. They had snapped off at the gums.

He felt lousy, but Sylvia dragged him into a hamburger saloon and ordered two portions of hamburgers and french fries.

Eddie shuddered at his and pushed it away. She toyed with hers, not actually eating.

Eddie said: 'All right — if you've something up your sleeve, spring it.'

She waited until the waiter had gone back behind the counter. Then she laid her bag on the table. 'You feel pretty bad after that cowardly beating he gave you, don't you, Eddie?'

'I feel about as bad as I look — '

'Bad enough for you to want to hit back at him — hard?'

He nodded and said: 'I guess it is. What's your idea?'

She said: 'Rest your hand casually on my handbag — go on, it won't bite.'

He hesitated; then he obeyed. His hand rested across the table on the top of the bag. It was of stiff material, but he could feel the hard shape of something squat and steel within. He withdrew his hand suddenly. 'Now I *know* you're crazy!'

'I've been planning it all along. I had an idea his price would be too high the minute I learned he wanted to blackmail me.'

'You don't think I'd really do anything like that to get you out of your jam, do you?'

She said: 'It isn't *entirely* my jam. How about that smack you took — you said you were pretty sore about it!'

He said: 'Not *that* sore, lady! Not a chance. I'm not mad enough to want to kill him!'

She hissed: 'For God's sake, Eddie, be *careful*! Don't shout!'

He frowned and lowered his voice. 'If that's what you meant when you said 'if all else fails', I don't want any part of it. I knew you were a devil, but I didn't think you were that much of a devil!'

She allowed a faint sneer to part her lips. 'I suppose you've never murdered a man?'

His fingers clenched on the cloth. 'What makes you say that?'

She shrugged. 'You were in the army, weren't you?'

'I never got as far as Europe. Even if I had, it wouldn't have been *murder*.'

'Wouldn't it? I don't see that — whichever way you carve it, it comes out as killing. And to my mind killing and murder are synonymous.'

'I wouldn't expect you to understand. But it isn't the same.'

She said: 'Is Schaparelli any better than the men we were fighting? *Is* he?'

'The case is different. It doesn't matter what Schaparelli is. Besides — they execute people for murder — or didn't you know?'

She smiled slowly. 'If they're caught.'

He shook his head. 'I want no part of it.'

She moved her hand so that it was laid across his. Her knees, under the table, pressed gently against his. She said: 'All right, Eddie. Don't shoot him yourself. *I'll* pull the trigger. *I'll* hold the gun. Just come along with me in case anything goes wrong. Will you?'

'And be as guilty, in the eyes of the law, as you will be? No thanks — I've had all the trouble I want up to now.'

'You're afraid!' she taunted.

'Maybe I am. But count me out.'

She got up slowly. 'Very well, Eddie. I'll do it myself.' She walked to the door. He jumped to his feet and came after her. He caught her up outside and gripped her arm savagely.

'I've threatened to walk out before — I haven't had the will power. But if you do this, I'll go! I mean it this time!'

They were far from the nearest street lamp. And she suddenly threw her arms about him, pressing him close to her. 'Help me out in this, Eddie. It wouldn't be murder, killing Schaparelli. You know

154

what he is. Help me this once ... Remember what we agreed ... ?' Her breath was warm and fragrant on his cheek. Her hair was against his nostrils, filling them with some subtle perfume she wore.

The warm life of her was pulsating against him; he pulled her madly to him and whispered: 'Forget Schaparelli, Sylvia ... '

'In the face of those photographs, Alex will throw me right out. He'll ... '

'Never mind Alex. Come with me. Let's get away from here. I'll make some money, somehow. Enough to buy you all you want, to take you anywhere you want to go — '

She shook her head. 'I want to, darling. But I daren't — I'm afraid of poverty. I've seen so much of it. I daren't take any chances. No matter how much I love you.'

He said: 'You *do* love me? You *mean* that?'

She pressed even closer. 'More than anything, Eddie. More than anyone I've ever met, or am likely to meet. But ... '

'But you love money more?' he said bitterly.

She seemed to slump. 'I can't help it, Eddie. I need to be secure.'

He said: 'All right. I'm going. I think you're still using your sex on me. I can see through you. I know you're pulling a line — I'm not biting. I'm getting out of town. I'm not coming back. Goodbye, Sylvia. You're *still* a bitch!'

She released him suddenly. Calmly she said: 'Very well, Eddie. You don't want to get tangled up with a cheap woman like me. But you'll *remember* me. You'll kick yourself for not staying. You'll realize what you missed.'

He grated: 'Don't get dramatic. There's been nothing between us to make me feel that way.'

She said: 'It isn't what's *been*. It's what *might* have been that's going to have you calling yourself a stupid fool. So long, Eddie.'

He said: 'Maybe I will have some regrets. But I've dangled from that string you've got me on long enough. I'm cutting loose now. I'm no puppet.' He turned suddenly and started walking in the opposite direction. His brain was whirling. Her white, appealing face seemed to have locked itself permanently into the front of his consciousness. He looked round once, and she was no longer there. His steps became slower and slower . . .

Sylvia walked along quickly. She gained the entry that led to the back of the Hole In The Wall. She turned down it, went a few yards, then waited.

She didn't have very long to wait. Within two minutes, hurried steps approached and turned at the entry. Then he had her in his arms again and was holding her as tightly as he could without breaking her ribs. He stammered: 'I *tried* — damn it, I *tried*! But I don't think I ever could leave you. I'm cooked.'

She murmured against his lips: 'I knew you wouldn't go, Eddie. We were meant to stay together. Don't leave me again, Eddie. Ever.'

He mumbled huskily: 'I won't, baby. I won't.' His lips clung to her neck just below the ear. And over his shoulder she smiled into the darkness. That unpleasant smile.

After a time he broke and said: 'You're determined to go through with it?'

She nodded. 'Did you notice anything about the back door of the place when they threw you out?'

'I'm afraid not. I was too groggy.'

'I did. I noticed particularly how the door fastened and everything. I took care to notice, because I had this plan in mind the minute they started hustling me through the back passage.'

'So?'

She kept her voice low. 'The yard door's bolted on the inside, but the wall isn't very high — you can climb it without much trouble. Then let me in. The back door to the club operates on a cheap type of lock. A fool could get in provided he had a penknife to force the catch back with. I suppose Schaparelli doesn't expect anyone to think of breaking into the club through his private quarters. Once we've got so far it's plain sailing. There isn't any lock on the inner

door. That leads into his living room
. . . we'll wait until he's in bed, and
then — '

Eddie said: 'I suppose you know how to
get to the bedroom without any trouble?'

'If he still uses the same room as he did
when I was single,' she agreed. 'It opens
off the living room. We won't give him the
chance to shout — the gun is fitted with a
silencer. It belongs to Alex, but he doesn't
have any use for it. I took it from his
bureau.'

He muttered: 'Can't we just hold him
up and demand the photographs?'

'No! He's too dangerous, Eddie. He
could have two or three sets of photographs, in addition to the negatives,
stowed away somewhere. When we've
— killed him, we'll have to search the
place thoroughly.'

'Is he alone on the premises when the
club closes?'

She said: 'In view of the number of
ladies he entertains, I imagine he is. He
wouldn't want anyone hanging round.'

'Not even a — photographer?'

'Not so late.'

Eddie shook his head doubtfully. 'You're forgetting the two thugs who helped him to hammer me, and who hustled you out. Mightn't they know about the blackmail? They know *I'd* have a good reason for wanting to kill him — and they most likely know who you are. Mightn't they tell the police, or something?'

She smiled. 'We'll have to take a chance on that. But my own opinion is that once the police start investigating, they'll find so much out about Schaparelli that they didn't know before — including the fact that he's a blackmailer — that his men won't be exactly anxious to mention that they had a hand in his dirty games.'

'But even if they keep quiet, won't they be looking for us, to — give us a little present?'

'I doubt that, too. Maybe they don't know just who we are. That might be information Schaparelli wants to keep to himself. But even if they do know, it's quite likely they won't associate us with the killing. There must be a thousand folks with reasons for wanting that swine dead. Why should we be singled out?'

'Because of what already happened tonight . . . '

She said: 'If I'm any judge of a rat's psychology, those two toughs will get out of town the second they find their boss is dead, in case they get tied up in the murder.'

Eddie said: 'You seem to have everything worked out. Now all we have to do is get in!'

'That'll be easy . . . will you take the gun, Eddie — or shall I?'

'Better hand it to me, honey.'

She gave it to him. He handled it with an expert hand. She noted that fact with interest. He took hold of her again, kissed her, and held it for a long time. He murmured: 'The things you get me into — but I'm not sure you aren't worth it, kid.'

She stole a glance at her wristwatch. 'It's after twelve, Eddie. We have about an hour or so to wait. How about some coffee?'

'Swell, but some place not too close. We

don't want to be seen in the vicinity. Can't take chances. Let's go.'

* * *

It was half past two by the time they reached the entry again. They had lingered unobtrusively on the sidewalk in the shadows and watched the staff of the club leave for the night, including the two thugs. Now, the club should be deserted — except for Schaparelli.

Sylvia led the way back to the rear door. The town was quiet. Along the top of the wall a black cat glided noiselessly.

Eddie said: 'I think they're unlucky.'

'This one is — for Schaparelli,' she hissed vindictively.

They took careful stock of the entry. It was silent and empty. Sylvia said: 'It should be all right now. Go on, Eddie.'

He hesitated for a moment; then he jumped, got his fingers to the top of the eight-foot wall and hung there. She gave him a shove up, and he gradually gained the parapet, keeping bent double as a precautionary measure. He paused to

162

regain his breath, then dropped silently inside the wall. The greased bolt of the door did not squeal as he drew it back. The door slid open a foot and Sylvia inched through. They stood in the darkness, breathing hard. There was no moon; no light of any description.

Eddie said: 'We have to get to the rear door without barging into any of these bottles or barrels. So be careful.' He started moving across the yard; she followed, holding on to the tail of his coat with one hand and feeling her way with the other.

They reached the door and Eddie fumbled cautiously for the handle, which he soon found. He said: 'How do I see to try to force the lock with my knife in this darkness?'

Sylvia murmured: 'Here, give me the knife. I think I remember where it is, exactly. Let me try.' Almost ten minutes passed, broken only by the scratching of the knife blade as she tried to force the sloping side of the catch back into the lock. Then she muttered triumphantly: 'Got it!'

Eddie pushed her gently aside and opened the door inch by inch. Then they slipped into the passage and down it. He was aware of Sylvia almost at his heels, although she made no sound.

They negotiated the passage in safety and stood before the door that led into Schaparelli's living room. The door that was without a lock. Sylvia breathed: 'Can you hear anything? Listen.'

They listened. There was no sound. Eddie gripped the handle of the door quietly, then turned. Moving fractionally, it opened under his careful hand. The room was in darkness. He edged forward, stood aside and waited for Sylvia to come through. In a moment she had joined him; her hand was touching his. Neither of them spoke.

Eddie stiffened suddenly. Across the room was another door. And within the room footsteps could be heard, moving about. He whispered: 'Is that the bedroom?'

'That's it.' Her hand gave a warning pressure. The door handle of the bedroom had made a squeaking noise as it was turned. Then it opened, an oblong of light streaming across the room.

They froze to the wall and waited.

A figure appeared in the doorway. It was Schaparelli. He muttered: 'Could have sworn I heard voices in here . . . '

Sylvia gave Eddie a nudge. She breathed: 'Now — shoot him, you fool! *Now!*'

Eddie remained still. Now it came to the actual killing, he was squeamish. His gun hand refused to operate.

Schaparelli had caught the sound of her voice. Now he barked: 'Who the hell's there — ?' He started to come forward.

Eddie felt the gun suddenly ripped from his grasp. There was a sudden blinding orange glare, followed by a soft, sinister plop — and a strangled cry from Schaparelli. Then Sylvia fired again, and again.

Her hand found a light switch nearby and clicked it on.

The club owner was on the floor, face down. He was bleeding profusely from the head. His arms were flung out. In one hand was a revolver. Obviously he had been alarmed by the voices, and had been about to do something drastic.

Sylvia said: 'Why didn't you fire, you fool? He might have shot us both down if I hadn't had the presence of mind to grab the gun!'

Eddie was abashed. He didn't speak. He was still too numb from the suddenness of it all.

And at that moment, in the open bedroom doorway appeared a fair-haired girl, wearing only undergarments. Her features showed her alarm. She began: 'What was that, dear? I — ' then she saw the body and the blood and, simultaneously, saw the two intruders. Her mouth opened for a scream — it was never uttered. Sylvia had taken rapid aim and fired, almost before the scantily dressed girl had opened her mouth.

Eddie groaned: 'Why did you have to do *that*?' He was horrified, dazed.

Sylvia stood where she was, staring down at the body of the girl. Then she observed: 'It's lucky I'm a good shot. At least she didn't suffer.'

Eddie was shocked at her callousness.

He said angrily: 'That kid never did you any harm! Why did you shoot her down like that?'

Sylvia shrugged. 'Don't be silly, Eddie. We can't afford to have any eye-witnesses. And how was I to know he'd have one of his doting females in here tonight?'

Eddie shook his head hopelessly. He crossed to the girl and bent down. Sylvia cautioned him: 'Don't touch anything that might take fingerprints, Eddie.'

He turned her over by the shoulder. The bullet had found a resting place almost centrally between her eyes.

He went to Schaparelli. He was dead, too. Two bullets had taken him in the head and face. He looked a mess. Eddie turned him over on his face again with a shudder.

Sylvia said: 'You haven't been much help so far. At least you can help me to find those photographs. We'll start in the bedroom.'

They both wore their gloves. They searched rapidly, not omitting anything. They tried the chest of drawers first, then the wardrobe and the tallboy. Sylvia even turned up the mattress on the bed without discovering anything.

She turned at last. 'They don't seem to be here.'

Eddie said: 'Where else is there?'

She said: 'His office, over the other side of the club. You try there whilst I try the living room. Take his key ring with you — it's there, on the dressing table.'

He took it and went through the door into the ghostly deserted club itself. By the aid of a match he worked his way over to the office door she had pointed out. He found a key that fitted and went in.

There was little in there to search: a desk, without any drawers locked; a filing cabinet, which contained items mostly relating to the club and its business; and a small briefcase. Within ten minutes he had exhausted the possibilities of the office. He left, relocking the door behind him.

Sylvia said: 'Let me have those keys, Eddie. I've found a metal deed box in the cupboard that looks as though it may be what we want.'

The deed box was long and rectangular. He gave her the keys and at the fifth attempt the lock snapped open. Quickly she opened the lid.

Inside were about fifty photographs. She worked through them eagerly. When she rose she held half a dozen photographs and three negatives in her hands. 'These are mine.'

'Perhaps he has more cached somewhere about,' Eddie suggested.

'We'll make another search. It wouldn't do to miss any.'

Half an hour later they halted. Eddie said: 'That seems to be the lot. Let's get out of here — we'll throw these on the fire first.' He indicated the other photographs.

Sylvia said quickly: 'No. Don't do that. Leave them. The police will suspect every one of *them*, then.'

'Don't be a fool. The first thing they'll realize is that if any of those people did it, they'd have taken care to remove their *own photographs*! If we burn the lot it'll help to confuse the police, because they won't know that he was a blackmailer.

They'll be puzzled as to the motive for the crime.'

She saw the sense of that. Then she looked curiously at the gun Schaparelli had been drawing, and said: 'Isn't that a thirty-eight?'

He picked it up, examined it, and nodded. She said: 'I've got an idea, Eddie! An idea that may even satisfy those two ugly swine you say might be after us.' She pointed to her own gun. '*This* is a thirty-eight. Now if I were to place this gun in the girl's hands, as if she had shot herself . . . after shooting Schaparelli . . . the police might think that she'd had trouble with him, had stolen his gun, killed him, then committed suicide!'

Eddie said: 'It's worth a try, I suppose. I haven't much faith in it, though.'

Nevertheless, Sylvia contrived to clench the dead girl's hand about the gun. Then she stood back and admired her handiwork whilst Eddie piled the incriminating photographs on to the fire. At length he was finished. He stood up.

'Have you burnt them *all?*' she demanded.

He nodded silently. He was still feeling shaken. He hadn't realized she was as ruthless as this.

'Then we'd better leave. Sure you haven't left any fingerprints anywhere?'

'I haven't taken my gloves off since we came in the yard,' he told her.

'And you've tidied the office after you? No one would think it had been ransacked?'

'No.'

Sylvia relocked the empty deed box and stowed it away where she had located it. She said, with satisfaction: 'No reason the police should suspect anything other than a love affair gone wrong, now.'

Eddie grunted: 'Let's get out. This place gives me the screamin' meemies!'

They left the way they had arrived. The rear door closed on its automatic lock. Sylvia went out cautiously into the entry. Eddie shot the back yard door bolt again, then climbed the wall.

They didn't go anywhere near the main street. Sylvia took him through dark and deserted side streets, entries, alleys, until they reached the edge of the town and the road leading to Garwood. It was not until then that they paused to consider the question of transport.

'The buses have stopped running,' she said. 'How are we going to get back?'

Eddie cursed. 'Why didn't we *think* of that! We can't walk, can we?'

'Hardly. It's more than fifty miles.'

'How about putting up at an hotel again?'

She said, reflectively: 'I don't know — I didn't like the way Alex acted the last time we were out the whole night. And we haven't any car to say we had a breakdown this time. No, Eddie. I think we'll have to risk taking a taxi.'

He wasn't too keen. He felt it was too obvious a lead. But she pointed out that there was no reason for the police to suspect them in any case. At last he saw it her way, and made a call from a phone box.

The taxi arrived within fifteen minutes — fifteen minutes which passed without either of them speaking. Eddie had not yet got over seeing the way she had coolly killed two people, one of whom she had not even known. Sylvia was busy congratulating herself that everything had gone smoothly. As far as her conscience was concerned, she felt no qualms whatsoever. It had been, she told herself, a case of self-preservation.

The taxi driver, although he was supposed to be an all-night operator, didn't eye them too kindly. He grunted: 'Where'd you wanna go?'

Sylvia said: 'There's a house about five miles past Keller's Crossroadhouse. Will you drop us there, please?'

'It's outta city limits, an' it's three in the mornin',' he pointed out. 'Cost you fifteen bucks.'

She said: 'That's all right. I'll give you twenty.'

They got in, and he drove away. As they went, he said: 'You birds surely rile me. You go out hottin' it up at some party an' then root hard-workin' cabbies out to take you home at three in the mornin'!'

Eddie snarled: 'You're operating an all-night service, aren't you?'

That shut the cabby up. He dropped them at the Crossroadhouse and took his money, then drove away. Eddie said: 'Why'd you tell him to drop us here?'

'I didn't want him to know we were from Garwood. We can walk the rest of the way. It isn't more than two miles now.' She held on to his arm and, keeping to the shadows, they began walking.

8

Doctor Webster laid aside his morning paper and looked irritably at the clock. Annie was clearing away his breakfast things. He said: 'Annie, isn't the mistress up yet?'

'I think she's getting up now, sir.'

'And Eddie?'

'He's been up a long time. I saw him go out for a stroll about an hour ago.'

She carried the tray out and Doctor Webster returned to his paper. But his mind was not on the printed words. He hardly saw the banner headline, which read:

TWO DIE IN FASHIONABLE NITERIE.

His mind was occupied with what, to him, was a graver matter. He had been prepared to believe Sylvia's story the first time she had stayed out the night. But for

175

it to happen *again* . . .

There was a light step at the door and Sylvia came in. She looked quite fresh and bright and pretty in a muslin dress of many colors. She came right over and kissed his forehead and he laid aside the paper.

'Good morning, darling!'

He replied: 'Good morning,' a little stiffly.

She said: 'Where's Annie? I'm starved.'

Annie came in with the tray and set out her breakfast. She said: 'Could you tell me when Mr. Martin will be in for his breakfast?'

Sylvia raised her brows. 'In? Why, is he out?'

'I saw him go out some time ago.'

'Then how should I know, Annie? You should have asked him. Anyway, you can keep it on a hotplate.'

Annie went out again, and Sylvia attacked the eggs. Webster laid aside his paper and watched her narrowly for a time. At length he said:

'Sylvia . . . you were rather late last night.'

She nodded. 'I know I was, dear. We missed the bus.'

He said: 'I waited up for you until after one before going to bed. I heard you letting yourself in at four-fifty by my watch. Where the deuce had you been until that hour?'

She said: 'It was really your *own* fault, Alex. If you hadn't wanted the car yourself, we should have been back quite early. I bet you didn't use it after all, did you?'

'As a matter of fact, I didn't. But I can't quite see what the car has to do with it.'

'It's really quite simple. You know what women are when they get gossiping. I had to tell her all about what a perfectly wonderful dear I'd married, and she had to tell me all about her own marriage and what she'd been doing since she left Garwood, and what she was likely to do in the future . . . I think I told you last night, when she called, what a terrible gossip she was — one of those people you simply *can't* get away from.'

She noticed he was eyeing her peculiarly. He said: 'Who was it you went to see? This friend of yours?'

She said: 'Why, Jenny Baxter, of course.'

'That isn't what you told me last night. Last night it was Milly Blake!'

She bit her lip. 'You certainly have a sharp memory, haven't you? Are you deliberately trying to make me a liar?'

'I'm not deliberately trying to do anything. But I think you ought to explain more fully — if that's possible.'

'Of course I can explain!' Sylvia pouted. 'You're being perfectly horrible . . . you say I spoke about Milly Blake last night — it's quite true, I did. Now I've mentioned Jenny Baxter. That's quite right, too. Milly Blake *is* Jenny Baxter! They're one and the same.'

He murmured: 'I still don't see — '

'Let me finish, Alex. Her full name used to be Mildred Jane Blake. That was *before* she married, when I knew her. Now she's *Mrs. Baxter*, and her husband appears to have a dislike for the name of Mildred, so he always calls her Jane, or

Jenny. With hearing him call her that all last night it stuck in my mind. I might equally have called her Milly Baxter. What does it matter?'

'But why did you call her Blake last night, when she called?'

'For the simple reason that I had no idea of her married name then, silly. I didn't learn that until I was introduced to her husband, later last night.'

He looked hard at her; her gaze was wide, innocent, slightly hurt and reproachful.

He suddenly mumbled: 'I'm sorry, Sylvia. I was afraid — '

'You know I wouldn't lie to you, Alex. And have I ever done anything you didn't want me to do since we were married?'

'No, of course you haven't.'

'Then aren't I entitled to a little trust?'

'I spoke without thinking. I'm sorry, Sylvia.'

'And you understand now why I wasn't back? Because we missed the last bus, hadn't the car, and had to root about for a taxi late at night — or, rather, in the morning.'

'You took a taxi then?'

'We did, darling. It was expensive, too.' She broke off as Annie came silently to the table and set the coffee down. She drank only one cup, then rose. 'I'm a little bit hurt, Alex. I'm going on to the porch if you've any more cross-examining to do.' She walked out without another glance at him.

He was gazing after her when he became aware of Annie at his elbow. 'I beg your pardon, sir . . . '

'What is it, Annie?'

She seemed nervous, but said: 'I was awake when the mistress came back last night, sir. I saw her and Mr. Martin come in.'

'What of it?' he snapped, irritably.

'Nothing, sir — except I heard the mistress say they came in a taxi — but they didn't, sir. They came walking, through the woods. I'd swear there wasn't any taxi.'

He didn't allow his expression to betray his feelings. 'Mrs. Webster has explained about last night. Just why are you so anxious to tell me these little things about her? You've always done it, Annie, ever since I married her. She says you don't like her — you make things up about her. Is that true?'

'No, sir. It isn't true. But I — I admit I don't like her, sir,'

'Why, Annie?'

Annie flushed faintly. 'I — it's just that I didn't think you made a wise choice, sir.'

'Don't you consider that's *my* affair, Annie?'

She said: 'I'm sorry, sir, honestly. But I don't want to see her make a fool of you, sir. I hate her when she lies to you — because I think so much of you, sir. She isn't a fit woman for any man, she's a devil — !'

'*Annie!*'

She broke off, confusedly. He told her gently: 'I appreciate your thinking so much of me, Annie. We've got along splendidly together, you and I. But it isn't your place to say things like that about your mistress. If Sylvia says she took a taxi, and yet you saw her walking, I daresay she has some very good reason for it. I know you're bitter — we were quite self-sufficient, you and I, before I married. You were a good housekeeper. I know you resented her intrusion, and to a certain extent I made allowances for you. But I hoped you'd change, and you'd grow to love her, as I do. Instead of that you're growing more bitter towards her. Annie, it will have to stop. At once. You are a servant here, after all, no matter how favored. And as such you have no right whatever to criticize your employer's wife so freely. If you don't like that state of affairs, then you can always give notice.'

The flush died from Annie's features, leaving them white. 'Oh, *no*, sir! I don't want to leave here — you. I'm sorry if I said anything wrong. I won't again, I swear.' She was very close to tears, and he softened.

'I know you thought you were acting for the best. I don't want you to go, Annie, but unless you cease to harbor these outrageous suspicions, you'll have to, I'm afraid. Now don't upset yourself — we'll forget this whole incident — and you forget about your mistress. Rely on me to look after my own interests.' He stood up and patted her shoulder. 'Off you go. And — thanks, anyway, for doing what you thought best.'

Annie sniffed miserably and went out. Doctor Webster stood staring after her for a long time. Then he picked up a table knife and began to twist it slowly between his fingers.

He went on to the porch at last, carrying his paper. Sylvia was there, and now she had been joined by Eddie. The doctor sat down in the cane chair usually reserved for his somewhat plump rear, and started to read. But he was haunted by Annie's words that Sylvia had not arrived in a cab.

Eddie and Sylvia had ceased talking with his approach. Perhaps they were being courteous and had shut up to give him a chance to concentrate on his paper. Perhaps.

He said, suddenly: 'By the way, Sylvia, one thing's been puzzling me . . . '

'Really, dear? Am I in the witness stand *again*?'

He felt belittled before Eddie. But Eddie seemed not to have heard. He was resting in a rocking chair, leaning forward with an elbow on the rail of the veranda, gazing towards Garwood.

Webster said: 'It was about the taxi. I don't doubt that you told the truth about it — but — well, Annie happened to mention in casual conversation — '

Sylvia said: 'Do you usually enter into casual conversation with your servants, Alex?'

He said: 'Annie isn't just a servant, Sylvia.'

'She is as far as I'm concerned. She doesn't like me, Alex, she's jealous. The fact is, she's in love with you herself, and resents me being your wife.'

He grunted: 'That's nonsense — Annie doesn't know what love is. And anyway, why should she care for *me*?'

'Don't make that mistake, Alex. Annie may be plain, but that doesn't mean she doesn't long for affection — probably more so than the average woman. She looked after you, cared for you, lived here alone with you until I came along . . . '

He was shocked. 'How can you think there was anything more than just a cordial relationship between that girl and myself?'

'I didn't say there was, dear. But Annie naturally began to feel you were her property. There wasn't any other woman. Then you married me — and the world she'd built up was shattered. She may even have hoped someday you'd forget how plain she was, and — well, I can't explain those hopes to you. I don't feel jealous of Annie — but I do object to her trying to estrange us by telling wicked stories.'

Her tirade had got home. He was subdued. He said: 'I expect it was just another lie.'

'What was it?' Sylvia demanded.

He laughed. 'Well, it was simply that Annie says she spotted you and Eddie *walking* home, from the direction of the woods. She says there wasn't any taxi.'

Sylvia frowned. 'So she's so keen on spying on me that she sits up and watches! The taxi driver only drove us as far as the junction of the road leading to

Garwood, Alex, if you wish to know. He *refused* to take us any further — he claimed the road up was so irregular and full of potholes that he daren't risk it on a moonless night. That's all there was to it. We hopped off and took the short way through the woods, past the pool.'

He nodded. 'I knew there was some reasonable explanation.'

Sylvia said: 'I can't understand you, Alex, placing any credence in the word of a someone like Annie.'

He was apologetic. 'I took her to task, dear. I told her if I was approached again with tales, I'd have to give her notice.'

Sylvia nodded. 'It would be wisest. I know she wants to split us up, darling. You'd see it, too, if you weren't so wrapped up in your work. But as long as you have the sense not to let her embitter you against me, I'll put up with it. I could put up with anything for your sake, Alex. You don't need me to tell you that.'

She got up and sat on his knee, with one arm about his neck. He patted her thigh. 'I know, darling. Forgive me if I seem unreasonable lately. I've been a bit overworked.'

'I'd forgive you anything, Alex. But promise me you won't listen to that foolish girl and her suspicions again?'

He said: 'I promise.' He looked at her wristwatch and said: 'It's late. I'll have to make a start on my rounds. Won't be back for lunch if I don't.' He waited until she slid from his knee after giving him a kiss. Then he threw the paper to Eddie. 'Read?'

Eddie, who had been silent and busy with his thoughts during the foregoing exchange, now snapped out of it and said: 'Thanks!'

Webster went inside. Eddie opened the paper. Sylvia returned to her chair.

Eddie said: 'It's in here — special edition. Must have found the body early. Let's see . . . Yes, it was discovered at five-thirty this morning by the char-women who went in to clean.'

She said: 'What do the police think?'

'Seems they've accepted it as a plain case of suicide following unpremeditated murder. The girl, it seems, was the wife of some banker in the town. Witnesses have turned up who say she was a reasonably frequent visitor at the club, although they were not aware she spent the night there.'

Sylvia said: 'I told you they'd think that!'

Eddie grunted: 'There's one thing you've forgotten, and I confess I didn't think of it myself at the time . . . that gun you placed in her hand! You say it was Alex's? Well, suppose they check on the number and find out to whom it was issued? What happens then?'

She laughed. 'You don't imagine I'm so big a fool as to leave a gun that might be traced to my husband, do you? Alex bought that gun when we were married — just afterwards. He said it was for me to use, if anything went wrong whilst he was out on night calls. He told me which drawer it was in in the bureau, and told me to go straight for it and not to be afraid to use it if anyone tried to break in or anything like that. He picked it up whilst I was with him, in town. At a second-hand shop. I doubt if the original license is even in existence.'

'He didn't license it, then?'

'No. I think he meant to, but it slipped his mind.'

'How about the one *you* took? Schaparelli's gun?'

'I'll put that back in the bureau in case he does remember he had a gun.'

'You can't do that. From what I saw of the two guns, they're quite different types.'

She smiled. 'Alex won't notice that even if he does look. As long as he finds a thirty-eight he'll be satisfied.'

Eddie shrugged. 'You know best.'

She said curiously: 'Where have you been this morning?'

He threw the paper aside with a moody grunt. 'Walking — in the woods. I couldn't sleep. Call me squeamish if you want . . . '

'About last night? Yes, I would call you squeamish. Schaparelli only got what he deserved. And we're perfectly safe.'

'It isn't Schaparelli. That girl — that's the part I can't get over.'

Sylvia murmured: 'She had to go. I'm not worried.'

He muttered: 'We don't think quite alike, you and I. Physically, we're attracted — mentally, it's something else again.'

She said: 'I thought you said you loved me?'

'I do love you — a love of the flesh that forms the frame you present to the world. Not of the mind and soul behind the body. I detest that.'

'You aren't very flattering, are you?'

'I don't intend to be, now or ever. I admit I haven't the mental power necessary to throw you out of my mind. This spell you've cast over me holds me fast enough. But I hate you for the way you treat your husband. I like Alex. I loathe you for the way you shot down that girl. And it makes me sick when you act like an innocent schoolgirl with that husband of yours!'

'Jealous?'

'Hardly! You give him a worse deal than you've given me so far. At least it's better to love you and know what you are, than to worship you and have no idea how coarse and rotten you are inside.'

'You aren't any little tin God, are you?'

'I don't pretend to be what I'm not,' he retorted sulkily.

She murmured meaningfully: 'Then you'd better. Because I was having a word with the local sheriff the other day, and he very much wants to see you to have a little chat.'

Eddie tautened. 'Why?'

She shrugged. 'How should I know? Perhaps he wants to sell you a ticket to the patrolmen's Thanksgiving party.'

Eddie seemed startled and ill at ease. He muttered: 'Why would he want to see me?'

She grinned. 'Don't be alarmed. Probably he merely wants to see if you're all right, as Alex claims. See if you really haven't suffered from the accident, or if we're trying to conceal something. He was told you were knocked down and couldn't make out why Alex failed to report, especially with Alex being the doctor here.'

'You think that's all?' Eddie said, breathing more easily.

'What else could it be? That and the

fact it really is part of his job to keep an eye on anyone who breezes into the district. But if you take a tip from me, you'll be careful — they aren't so cut off as they seem up here. For instance, the sheriff gets 'wanted' circulars from all over the country every month.'

Eddie started again, then eyed her uneasily. He said: 'Why should that worry me? I'm not frightened of your sheriff.'

'Then you aren't going to run out on me?'

'There's no reason I should run out that I know of. And even if there was, I wouldn't go. I helped you last night — you know our agreement. I'm holding you to that.'

She nodded. 'I've no intention of trying to bilk this time. The first night Alex is called out on a long case, we can make our arrangements.'

He said: 'It had better be soon.'

★   ★   ★

But it wasn't soon. By the whims of fate, Doctor Webster was not called out to any late night case for almost two months.

Summer turned to autumn, and autumn showed the first signs of approaching winter.

Annie watched, still . . .

Sylvia was as innocent as ever with Alex, as seductive as ever with Eddie.

The Schaparelli case seemed to have blown over . . . the Hoffenheim kids got over their measles safely . . . and the doctor didn't suggest that Eddie run Sylvia into town again — and Sylvia didn't ask him, perhaps thinking it would be wiser to go quietly for a time.

Eddie grew a moustache, which Sylvia suspected was entirely due to her hint about a possible visit from the sheriff. Yet, though the sheriff often called at the house with eggs and chickens, he made no effort to seek out the new hand.

Eddie went quietly about his work. He drove the doctor on his rounds several times. He tended to the small garden. He chopped wood for the winter and avoided going to the village as far as possible. But he didn't forget Sylvia's promise. He waited impatiently, his desire mounting with every passing week — with every provocative glance she gave him, and with every kiss she bestowed on the lined cheeks of her husband.

Winter came in with full force. An icy wind howled mournfully over Garwood. Torrential rain fell for four days running. The woods and the fields became soaking morasses. The pool was full to overflowing. No birds sang about the house on the rise. Alex was kept busy with cases of influenza, colds, chronic rheumatics, and sore throats and coughs.

Dead and withered leaves lodged in the garden and disintegrated into the earth under the heavy pressure of the rains. The trees thrust denuded branches into the black, screaming night, dripping with moisture that turned the mellowness of their trunks to jet black. Windswept raindrops pattered unceasingly on the veranda; they no longer sunned themselves in the chairs out there.

Garwood was pleasant enough in the summer; in the winter it was hell. But strangely, with each passing week, Eddie became more and more carefree, more at ease.

September gave way to October and November; the rain ceased and the ground hardened, but the nights were still dark and dismal. With the advent of the moon the woods were visible from the house, gaunt and ghost-like in the hard, clear light.

And whilst they sat at supper one night, the call came. Doctor Webster took it. When he returned to them, he looked grave.

'It's the Jacksons again, Sylvia. As I feared — the husband had 'flu, but still went out to feed the chickens and chop the wood when I'd expressly warned him not to. His wife shouldn't have let him, but — ' He shook his head, then went on: 'There've been rumors. I don't pay a great deal of attention to rumors, but I've seen Mrs. Jackson myself in the village. She always visits Jed Clay. He's a single man, and it isn't quite the thing. Unfortunately, she has that man of hers under her thumb. I believe she wants to get rid of him entirely. It's a hard thing to think of any woman . . . however, facts speak for themselves. The fellow's been out, probably at her insistent nagging, and now he's down and out. Most likely pneumonia. I may not be back very early — depends how bad he is. I'll let you know by phone, dear.'

Eddie cut in: 'I'll drive you along there, Doc.'

'No, no, Eddie. I won't drag you out on a night like this. I can manage quite well. You stay and see the house is all right. I never have liked leaving Sylvia alone, you know.'

Sylvia, as usual, kissed him lingeringly. 'Be careful, Alex.'

'Trust me. I may be home before you know it.'

He went, and they said nothing as they listened to the sound of the car engine warming up and combating the cold, sighing winds outside. They heard the backfire of the car, the sound of the wheels crackling out on to the trail. And then Eddie said: 'It looks as if this is it!'

Sylvia was silent still, straining to hear the last remote engine noises.

Then they heard another sound — that

of the front door being closed quietly. Sylvia uttered an exclamation and rose, then went into the passage. Annie was there. 'What are you doing with the door open, Annie?'

'I was watching the doctor go, Mrs. Webster,' she said sullenly.

'Why? There's no necessity for you to do so.'

'I'd given him a warmer for the car — and a flask of coffee in case he's there all night. I know he's fussy about the way his coffee's made. He might not like the way Mrs. Jackson makes it.'

Sylvia said softly: 'Sometimes you exceed your duties, Annie.'

Annie felt rebellious. 'I've always done it, Mrs. Webster, and I don't intend to stop just because *you* say so.'

Sylvia's voice was very quiet, silky almost. 'Go back to the kitchen, Annie. That's *your* place. If anyone sees my husband off, *I* will.'

Annie opened her mouth; thought better of it, and went. But her expression was malevolent.

Sylvia turned into the front room

again. 'It was Annie — sneaking about as usual.'

Eddie grunted: 'Never mind Annie. Remember what you said . . . '

'I haven't forgotten. But we don't know if Alex will be out for very long yet. He may come back.'

'If he is out any length of time?'

She muttered: 'About one o'clock. My room. For heaven's sake, be careful. If Annie should find out . . . You must be sure she's in bed before you — come.'

'I'll watch out for that. You really mean to play the game this time?'

' 'Play the game' is a rather awkward expression, isn't it? Let's say I mean to keep my promise this time. It's been rather boring for me here lately. Tonight something new will be added.'

He stood up to move over and sit beside her. She said: 'Wait. Not yet, Eddie. Don't spoil things.'

He sat down again without a word. But his blood was pumping faster through his veins.

Sylvia sat calmly at the piano. She played and sang 'Smoke Gets In Your

Eyes', 'Night and Day', and 'Frankie and Johnny'. She had a husky, pleasing voice, a voice full of sensuality.

The phone rang. She stopped and took it, listened, and said: 'Oh, what a pity, dear. I'm sorry.' She came back to the piano and resumed her singing.

Eddie said: 'Was that him?'

'Yes. Jackson won't last more than another eight hours or so. Alex is staying, to do what he can. He won't be home tonight.'

Eddie murmured: 'One o'clock!'

9

Somewhere in the Webster home, a clock struck one. Upstairs on the second floor, the passage was wrapped in gloom. From an end window, feeble moonlight strayed along past the four doors.

The second door from the window opened without a creak. Eddie looked out. He waited for a few seconds, then emerged and walked soft-footedly along to the door next to the window. Here he paused, half bent, until his ear was close to the keyhole. Inside the room he could distinguish the sound of regular and deep breathing. There was no movement.

He smiled to himself, turned — and blundered against a chair leg. He froze; the noise he had made had been insignificant. But he could afford to take no chances. For nearly two minutes he held his position, silent and motionless. Then he listened again. The deep, regular breathing inside the room continued.

Carefully avoiding the chair, he moved in stockinged feet down the passage, past the head of the stairs, past Doc Webster's empty bedroom, to the far door at the other end.

It was closed. A sudden suspicion hit him — that Sylvia might have tried the same game on him as she had at the hotel. He gripped the handle silently. It turned, and the door opened.

He moved inside. There was no light. Moonbeams wandered in at the wide window and fell across the woman in the bed. His breathing quickened. Her eyes were closed. He said: 'Sylvia!'

'Shhh!' She was awake then, waiting. She opened her eyes. 'Annie — ? You were careful?'

He nodded and said: 'I just came from her room. I could hear her breathing deeply. She's asleep.'

'You didn't make *any* noise?'

'A chair in the passage, but it didn't signify.'

She uttered a low exclamation. 'Annie's got terribly keen hearing! She probably heard you!'

'No she didn't. I waited, to make certain. She was still asleep.'

She murmured: 'Lock the door, Eddie. The key's in the lock. Then come over — but we mustn't drop asleep. Alex may be back at any time — Jackson may go suddenly. We must keep our ears open, and the second we hear his car in the roadway you must hurry back to your room.'

He twisted the key silently in the lock, and then moved eagerly towards the bed . . .

★　★　★

Annie was late going to bed that night. She waited until both Sylvia and Eddie had retired to their respective rooms. It wasn't that her work kept her late — but she had other things on her mind.

She sat in the kitchen and waited patiently. At eleven Sylvia looked round the door. 'Not in bed, Annie?'

'I don't feel very sleepy.'

Sylvia yawned. 'I do — good night.'

Annie said: 'Good night, Mrs. Webster.'

Sylvia went. Annie sat on. At about eleven-thirty Eddie wandered in. 'Still burning the midnight oil, Annie?'

'It isn't midnight yet, Mr. Martin.'

He smiled. 'Isn't it about time you cut that Mr. Martin? I told you a long time ago that I'm like you — just a servant here. Eddie to everyone, and that includes you.'

She said: 'You're more like one of the family.'

'So are you, Annie. Well, as long as you're up, how about a cup of coffee?'

'There's one in the pot, sir. I just now made it.'

He poured coffee and splashed cream in liberally. Then he sat opposite her and smiled. He sipped his coffee slowly. 'You shouldn't miss your beauty sleep, Annie.'

He saw her wince, and felt awkward. 'I shouldn't, should I? *I* need it.'

He thought it best not to make matters worse, and changed the subject. 'I'll be pushing along, I think. Fifteen minutes to twelve — time I was in bed. 'Night, Annie.'

'Good night — Mr. Martin ... you ...'

He paused at the door. 'Yes?

'I was just going to ask if you wanted a — a bedwarmer.'

He smiled inwardly. 'No, thanks. I'm toughening myself up. Good night.'

He went out and left her sitting on. It was almost twelve-thirty before she switched off the light and made her way upstairs. In her hands she carried a reel of thin black cotton.

She paused outside Eddie's room. She didn't like doing this to Mr. Martin — he was nice. But her affection for Webster over-rode her faint liking of Eddie. It had to be done. If he'd allowed that woman to get a hold on him he had only himself to blame. She had warned him when first she'd learned he was going to stay.

She took the loose end of the cotton, made a loop, and tied it gently about the door handle. Then she led the rest of the reel along by the wall to her own door. She unrolled a fair length and snapped it from the reel, which she placed in her pocket. That done, she threaded the loose end through her keyhole, went inside, and closed the door softly behind her. She found the end and took it carefully to her bedside.

She didn't undress. She got under the clothes as she was, and tied the end of the cotton taut about her middle finger. She knew that if Eddie's door was opened from either outside or inside, the cotton would pull before it snapped. And no one would notice it in the shadowy passage.

The clock below struck the half-hour. The house seemed very silent, almost as if it was listening for something itself. She didn't sleep; she was thinking.

There was a sudden, almost imperceptible tug at her finger. Then the cotton went slack!

Annie began to breathe as she would if she'd been asleep. She didn't move yet. Minutes dragged by. There was a sudden faint noise as if a chair had scraped slightly in the passage. It was not repeated. But Annie continued to lie still, to breathe evenly. Her hand was tight about the thin shred of the slack cotton. She gave the prowler ten minutes to get clear before she slid one black stockinged leg softly to the floor. Her slippers were by her feet, but she did not put them on.

She opened her door a fraction and stared into the passage, accustoming her eyes to the gloom. The passage was deserted. She went right out, re-closing her room door, and trod along to the door of Eddie's room. For a minute she paused; then, screwing her courage together, she turned the handle slowly and opened the door.

She didn't need to go any farther into the room to see that the bed was unoccupied. Her heart hammered under her plain black dress.

She went out again and started to slide stealthily along the passage, moving her lame leg as noiselessly as she could, past the head of the staircase and along to Sylvia's door, where she halted to listen.

She could distinguish nothing when she bent to the keyhole. The key was in the lock, and she guessed the door would be locked. But she heard breathing and, once, the creaking of a bed.

She stood up again; she had to know

for certain Eddie was in that room with Sylvia! Then she'd be able to face Webster and acquaint him with the true facts, which she had seen with her own eyes. She'd risk his wrath then, and could face Eddie and Sylvia with her story if called upon to do so. She didn't think for a moment that Eddie could be anywhere other than in that room; but there was a faint possibility that he was out of the house, and had gone for a late night walk alone. She had to know for certain.

She waited and listened for nearly fifteen minutes. No other sounds rewarded her vigil. Then she retraced her steps as far as the staircase and went down it rapidly to the kitchen door, then out into the chill winter night. The wind caught her clothing, whipping her plain dress tight about her thin, stick-like legs as she hurried to the shed. The cold struck up and through her stockinged feet, sending a paralyzing nerve pain along her injured leg. But she scarcely noticed it. Straight hair flying out behind her, like an avenging Valkyrie, she gained the shed door and went inside.

When she emerged she carried a short ladder — short, but long enough to reach the second-floor windows! Eddie used it for cleaning them; she planned to use it for something vastly different. Stumblingly, she carried it across to the front of the house. The moonlight was strong here, bathing everything in a mellow, cheese-colored glow. She stared anxiously up and down the trail; there was no one, nothing, to observe her next actions.

It took all her frail strength to rear the ladder slowly and quietly; but she accomplished it, driven on by her intense hatred of the woman who had cut her so completely out of the doctor's life and thoughts.

Then she essayed the climb. It involved considerable risk. Her leg would not bend at the knee, so her progress was painful and slow. Five minutes later she was immediately beneath the window of Sylvia's room. The ladder ended there. Now she had to inch upwards, using the wall of the house for handhold. The wind whirled her skirts again and tore at her slight form with savage vigor, as if it would wrench her from the ladder and hurl her down to serious injury; it was almost as if the wind was in connivance with the wrongdoers in that room.

Her feet found the next rung, and her hands clung to the wall . . .

* * *

Eddie relaxed. His left arm rested about Sylvia's slim waist; his lips clung to her white neck. Her eyes were closed. They were surfeited with wild lovemaking. She was everything he had told himself she would be. He raised himself on one elbow and gazed at her face by the penetrating moon-rays. He wondered, and forgot the characteristics about her that he hated.

At length he murmured: 'This — won't be the end?'

Her eyes remained closed. 'There won't be any end, Eddie. Not now.'

'You mean — ?'

'Whenever Alex is away — whenever it's safe. Perhaps, in the summer — there's the pool, and I know of a few secluded spots higher on the hill . . . kiss me, Eddie.'

He kissed her lingeringly, then said: 'Sylvia! Let's do what I said — let's leave, run away. I can find a job . . . '

'Don't spoil it now. I've told you why I won't leave with you. Let's not talk about that. We're both comfortable here.'

He said: 'But sooner or later we're sure to be found out! What then?'

She stirred uneasily. 'If we are, we can think of something. Let's not worry ourselves now.'

His lips closed on hers again.

She said: 'What time is it now, Eddie? We've been here a long time. I'm thinking that Alex may be on his way back. I'll see. If he's on the way I can spot the car headlights on the down road from the Jacksons' home.' She got up and began to cross to the window. She stiffened.

'*Eddie!*'

'What is it?'

Instead of answering, she quickened her steps towards the window, flung it open, and stared out. She saw something black scurrying away into the shadows,

210

and her lips tightened; her face became hard. 'Did you leave a ladder here under this window today?'

'Ladder? No. I haven't cleaned the windows since the bad weather.'

'There's one here now!'

He jumped from the bed and joined her.

She hissed: 'Annie! I knew it! Eddie — get dressed quickly and go to the Jackson home. See if you can help Alex . . . It's our only chance of establishing an alibi if Annie tells Alex what she's seen! She won't know you went for him, to drive him home. If she says you were with me he'll believe she's lying . . . Make some excuse to Alex. Say you didn't feel tired and thought he might be worn out and need you to drive him home. It's all we can do to protect ourselves. It may not work if he notices the time you arrive. But it's worth a try!'

Eddie saw the sense of it; he kissed her. 'I'll go. Don't worry!' He went back to his own room and dressed hurriedly. Ten minutes later Sylvia saw him leave the house and make for the trail.

She told herself it was lucky she'd caught Annie in the act. She left the room quietly. Her mouth was tight and cruel.

Meanwhile, Eddie forced his way uphill against the strong wind. Head down, coat buttoned close, he forged onwards.

If Annie did talk, it would naturally be better for him to have been part of the night with the doctor. He felt vaguely sorry for Annie.

The Jackson shack lay beyond some heavy climbing. It sheltered in an overhanging crag of the mountains. Jackson and his wife were farming people. They employed several hands from the village, and their own two ten-year-old kids did odd jobs about the place. They weren't exactly rich — the farm paid its way, nothing more.

The shack loomed up in the distance, and he could now see the doc's car standing outside it. The lights inside were off, though there was a porch light operating, casting a sickly yellow glow on the five wooden steps leading to the board veranda. He noticed that every blind in the place was fully drawn, and his lips twisted sardonically. Apparently the good Mrs. Jackson was anticipating the undertaker.

He found a bell-pull and tugged gently. Somewhere in the roomy shack a bell tolled. The door opened on a chain and the hard face of a hill woman peered at him. It was the wife. He didn't know her by sight, but after Webster's remarks he could guess it. She had a certain amount of plump attractiveness — of the kind that would appeal to the rough workers about the place. She might have been thirty-eight or forty-eight. He said:

'Good morning . . . I'm Eddie Martin, Doctor Webster's chauffeur. I came along to see if there was anything I could do for the doctor.'

She said shortly: 'There ain't. He's with my husband. He's dyin'. There ain't nothin' nobody can do now.'

'You don't mind if I have a word with the doctor?'

'Come in. You might as well.' She opened the door and stood aside whilst he entered. Then she shot the bolt again and swung the chain across. 'In there. It's all right . . . ' She indicated a door on the left. As Eddie went he caught sight of two children, a boy and girl, in their nightwear, seated on a pair of rough wooden chairs, white-faced and tense. Sitting near the fire in a cozy leather chair, toasting his booted feet at the blaze, was a surly-featured man, about the woman's age. He gave Eddie a curious look, but did not speak.

Eddie opened the room door and went in. Doctor Webster was by the bed, folding his stethoscope.

Mrs. Jackson said: 'How is he, Doctor?'

Webster shook his head. 'I'm afraid he's lower.'

She nodded. 'You can give me a call if he shows signs of goin'.' She went out, closing the door.

Webster viewed Eddie with some surprise. 'What brings you up here, Eddie? Nothing wrong, is there? Hasn't been another emergency call?'

Eddie shook his head. 'Everything's all right, Doc. I couldn't sleep and decided to take a walk. I walked around the hills — been walking for about two hours,

214

maybe more. Then I found myself outside here — recognized your car. So I decided I might as well see if I could help you.'

'That was good of you, Eddie. But I don't need any help — take a look . . . '

He moved aside and Eddie stared at the thin, gaunt form under the bed-clothes. The man was flushed; a fine sweat beaded his features. His thin, gnarled hands were clenched over the coverlet. His sparse gray hair was standing in spiky clumps on the crown of his head.

Eddie murmured: 'Well, I guess he's had his life, anyway.'

Webster shook his head. 'Dan Jackson's only forty-five, Eddie.'

Eddie felt shocked. 'But — '

'The way he looks? Overworked. Nagged at until he was driven almost out of his mind. She married him because he owned this place. Then she didn't want him. Usually I don't trust rumors; but in this case everything they say in the village is true. Jackson never had a chance. There wasn't a soul in the world cared for him — other than his two kids. There's no one here to cry over his deathbed . . . '

'How about the surly chap in the other room? Isn't he a friend?'

Webster smiled mirthlessly. 'That's Dan Jackson's worst enemy. Oh, they used to be friends, once. But Jed Clay coveted Jackson's money and farm. Clay's a local farmhand. He saw a way of getting it, too. Under the pretext of calling on Dan, he formed an alliance with Dan's wife. She used to visit him in the village. Dan got to know, but he was too cowed by his wife to do anything about it. I ask you, Eddie! Did you ever hear of anything more despicable than Clay's actions? Sitting out there now, waiting for his one-time friend to die, so that he can claim the wife and the farm! Can you believe it's humanly possible for anyone to behave like that? Accepting a man's hospitality and betraying his trust?'

Eddie felt queer, and gulped: 'Maybe it's all *her* doings — maybe she's got a grip on him that he can't break. Maybe he couldn't break away if he wanted to.'

Webster looked thoughtful. 'I hadn't thought of it that way, but I wouldn't put it past Jackson's wife.'

'She looks a hard type.'

'Hard as oak! In fact, she killed him! After my express orders that he was to stay in bed, she permitted him to go out in this weather. She knew what it would do to him — and most likely she *made* him. But we couldn't prove that . . . '

The gaunt frame on the bed stirred. The man whispered hoarsely: 'Sally . . . Sa — lly. Gi — give me y' — y'hand . . . '

Webster got up, went to the door and opened it. 'He's calling for you, Mrs. Jackson.'

'I'm making coffee — I'll come in about ten minutes.'

Webster shut the door again. He looked at Eddie and shrugged. The wasted figure on the bed breathed: 'Wh'are y'girl? Sal — '

Webster said: 'He's delirious — probably remembering her as she once was.'

Eddie said: 'Why doesn't she come?'

Webster didn't answer. He crossed and laid more logs on the fire. Webster turned from the fire and stared. Eddie was beside the bed. He had hold of the dying man's hand. His face was grave.

Webster said: 'That's decent of you, Eddie.'

Eddie said softly: 'If this'll ease the poor devil any . . . '

Webster sat on the other side of the bed and waited. 'When I see those two damned vultures waiting out there it makes me fume,' he said, his fingers clenching.

Eddie muttered: 'He's going hellish cold, Doc . . . '

Webster got busy. Then he went to the door again. 'Mrs. Jackson! You'd better come along in, now.'

Mrs. Jackson came in. She stood stiffly beside the bed, listening to her husband's muttering. She made no move to take his hand. She was impassive. The door opened again and Jed Clay thrust his head through. 'Poor ole Dan agoin'?'

Webster said: 'You'd better wait in the other room, Clay. Don't want anyone other than the family in here. You can send the kids in, if you will . . . '

Clay withdrew, scowling. The children came in, holding hands very tightly. Eddie felt a pang as he looked at their white, tear-stained faces and their thin little arms and legs which projected beyond the confines of their night attire. They stood beside their mother, afraid to move in the presence of death.

One strained hand stirred against the coverlet in an effort to move upwards. Then fell back.

Doctor Webster said: 'He's gone, Mrs. Jackson.' He bent over the recumbent figure.

The two kids burst into a wail of misery. The woman said, icily: 'Get ye back to bed — now!' They shuffled miserably from the death room. She followed them.

Webster looked up. 'He's dead, Eddie. Pass me that sheet.' He laid the clean sheet across the still figure. Then he sighed and passed a hand across his brow. 'I wanted to save him. I didn't want her to have her way. But there it is. There comes a time when the finest physician in the world can't do any good. That time came for Dan Jackson. He wasn't a bad fellow . . . ' He bowed his head for a moment and his lips moved slowly: 'Lord

God, I commend his soul to Heaven.'

Eddie said: 'Amen.' Then he followed Webster through into the other room.

Jed Clay was talking to Mrs. Jackson in low tones. Doctor Webster interrupted brusquely: 'You heard me inform you that Dan's dead, I take it?'

'Ay, I heard.'

'Then you ought to know that it's through your own neglect! If you hadn't driven him out into the cold — '

She flared up. 'Ye'll be gettin' y'self into trouble if ye aren't careful, Doctor Webster. What d'ye mean by sayin' I *druv* him out? I did no such thing . . . he wanted to go, an' go he did. I told him you said he wasn't to, but it didn't make no difference. He said 'e had his work to do.'

Webster shook his head. 'You could have stopped him.'

'I didn't think he was that bad.'

Webster said: 'It's liable to be a shock to the children. I'll just slip up and give them a sedative, if you don't mind.'

'I do mind. I want you out o' the house. Jed'll take care o' them — an' they'd better get used to the idea o' death, anyway. I ain't all lookin' for them to grow up soft . . . they'll have to do their hands' turn on the farm.'

Webster snapped his bag shut. 'Very well. I'll let Thomas Blare know Dan's dead.'

'I already told Blare. Yesterday. I had a feelin' Dan'd be goin' this time. Blare's started the coffin already.'

Eddie felt chilled. He opened his mouth to speak. Then shut it.

Webster said: 'I'll send in my bill.' Then to Eddie: 'Let's get along, Eddie.'

The woman came to the door with them. She shot the bolt and dropped the chain. They went out into the wind and heard the bolt rammed home again.

Webster muttered: 'By God, Eddie, I'd like to have that woman behind bars! She killed him as surely as if she'd driven a knife through his heart! But what can I do without proof?'

Eddie said nothing. The wind bit through his coat, freezing him to the bone. That night he had looked on the work of fiends.

They got into the car, and Eddie took the wheel. His hand was unsteady as they bumped on to the road. Webster said: 'Folks like you and I, and the people we know and love, can't understand people like that woman.' Eddie was silent. Webster continued: 'Don't mention this to — to Sylvia or to Annie, Eddie. They'd be shocked.'

Eddie husked: 'I won't say anything, Doc.'

They drove on in silence, and finally, as the dawn found a footing on the black reaches of the sky back of the hills, they reached the Webster home. Eddie hurried to garage the car; when he got in, the doctor had two tall glasses of brandy on the table.

'Drink that — warm you up. I think we deserve it.'

Eddie nodded numbly. The brandy coursed down his throat and sent warmth leaping through his veins. He said: 'I couldn't take your job, Doc. Things like that — what happened tonight — a few incidents like that would finish me.'

'It isn't that bad,' Webster said kindly.

'Think of the good you can do. Think of the folks round here — nearly twelve hundred of them — who look on me as a friend and helper. They rely on me for seeing them through all their illnesses. And, as a rule, I very seldom let them down. Take poor Annie, for example. That kid would have lost her leg — but for my belief that I could save it.'

Eddie shook his head. 'I still couldn't do it. I don't know why. I expect I'm just — squeamish.'

Webster said: 'Where other people are concerned, eh? I didn't notice anything squeamish about you when I was treating your broken leg, Eddie. You took it better than anyone I've attended.'

'That's different. It isn't so much physical pain I can't stand, as — well — I don't know, Doc. I can't explain it. It's just the circumstances that affect me. Like that poor guy snuffing out, calling for his wife — and that bitch already making the arrangements for the funeral and her remarriage. Ugh!'

10

It was almost ten before Eddie got down the following morning. Doc. Webster was out on his rounds. Sylvia was not in the morning room. He wandered about the house and found her in the kitchen, at a sink piled high with dishes. Her dainty dress was covered by one of Annie's old aprons, and her arms were plunged in greasy water to the elbows.

'Morning, Eddie. Your breakfast is on top of the plate. Didn't want to wake you up, considering the time you got home. Alex said to let you sleep.'

He found his breakfast and ate. Then he laid the dirty dishes on the draining board for her. 'I'll wipe.'

She indicated a towel and he started wiping. He said: 'Where's Annie?'

She smiled triumphantly: 'Annie's gone. Don't ask me why. The only thing I can think of is that she couldn't stand knowing what she did know and staying here to see Alex made a fool of. Perhaps she thought if she told him what she had found out he wouldn't thank her for it — anyhow, she went!'

'Where the hell could anyone like Annie make a fresh start?'

'I don't know, or care. I hope she winds up in the gutter, where she belongs. I was sick and tired of having her spying on me.'

He said: 'Maybe she just went for a short while, to think things over?'

'She took all her things — and left a note.' She pointed towards the table, and he laid aside the plate he was drying and went to read the note. It was printed in Annie's usual illiterate scrawl. Annie hadn't had much schooling, with one thing and another. It said:

★ ★ ★

Dere Doctor Webster,
  I can not stay under this roof one more nite knowing what I do know. I do not like leeving like I am, but I can not stay any more. Missus Webster dont like me

and I dont like her. You wont believe anything what I tell you, so I am going. If you new what I know you wuld throe her out.

I hoap everything will be allrite for you, Annie.

★   ★   ★

Eddie put the note down and said: 'What did you say to her last night after I'd left?'

Sylvia raised her eyebrows. 'I didn't have any hand in it, my dear. Please don't get the idea I threw her out.'

He put the ill-printed note down and resumed drying for her. She said: 'You realize what it means, don't you?'

He nodded hesitantly. 'It means we can pull the wool over your husband's eyes every time he's out, doesn't it? *Now*, if we were inclined!'

'How bright you are, Eddie boy.' She smiled. 'But you don't seem too pleased. I thought you'd have been delighted.'

He said: 'Last night I saw Jackson — Dan Jackson — die.'

'Alex told me about it.'

226

'He went whilst he was in a coma. But it was the way that death had been brought about. I saw his wife and Jed Clay — I never saw a more wicked-looking pair in my life. Alex thinks Jed Clay's to blame for it all. I know it was the woman . . . '

'What's that to do with anything?'

He said levelly: 'It made me think of you and me, Sylvia. It makes me wonder if you'll finish up like the Jackson woman, and if I'll finish up like Jed Clay!'

She sneered: 'You'd prefer to finish up like Jed Clay rather than like Dan Jackson, wouldn't you?'

He muttered: 'I'm not sure . . . '

She faced him. 'Remember this, Eddie. You either kick people around or get kicked around yourself. I'm not cut out to be kicked around. That's why I do the kicking. I don't know about you — but if you feel your character is attuned to leading the life of a Dan Jackson, we won't get along.'

He grunted: 'It's because I've allowed you to kick me around so much that we've got as far as we have. If I'd been a

Jed Clay I'd have either walked out, or kicked *you* around!'

She cut in: 'There are *millions* of wives doing what I'm doing. *Millions* of single men doing what you're doing. And just as many husbands being fooled as there are wives to fool. Why *should* we wind up like Mrs. Jackson and Jed Clay?'

'I didn't say we would. I just wondered — remember, that's how it started with Jackson. His friend, accepting hospitality, and then betraying him!'

She dried her hands on a towel and took his shoulders. 'It seems you've belatedly discovered a conscience, Eddie. You'd better have a quiet sit down and make your mind up.'

He grunted: 'One thing's certain. If I do decide to give Doc a straight deal, I'll have to get right out of your life.'

She spat out: 'Then get out of it, Eddie. If you feel like you say you do, get out right away!' She tore off the apron and threw it down. Without another word or look, she walked from the kitchen.

Eddie was angry at her for not trying to understand his feelings, after all he had put up with for her. At the cold tone of her voice, and the absolute lack of affection. It seemed she had no use for him, despite her remarks of the night before.

All right, he thought grimly, I'll go. And this time I *won't* come running back.

He had his things packed within ten minutes. He wanted to leave before the doctor returned. That would save awkward explanations. Leave it to her to cook up some story for Alex.

He had intended to leave without seeing her. But as he passed the front room he could hear her moving about. He went in. She was dusting and sweeping. He said: 'I expect you'll be in a hurry to get a new maid.' He didn't know what else to say.

'I'm taking over the cooking and housework myself from now on,' she told him coldly. 'I've arranged with Alex to do it. I don't want another Annie round the place. So you're going now?'

'Yes. I'm going.'

'Goodbye, Mr. Martin. I'll make your excuses to Alex.'

He wanted her to persuade him to stay even now. He put down the old leather case the doctor had given him and went towards her. She faced him coolly.

'Well, Mr. Martin?'

'Don't be like that. Why part like this? Surely, after — surely we can remain friends?'

'Of course we can. I feel quite — *friendly* — towards you.'

He reached out and imprisoned her in his arms, tried to kiss her. Her hand came up stingingly across his cheek.

His temper went and he forced her to him and pressed his lips against hers. Her warm, moist lips belied her attitude. But she pushed him away.

'If you've quite finished with me, I'll go on with my cleaning.'

He grabbed his case savagely. 'Then be damned to you!' he snarled, and went out, slamming the door after him.

He went on to the trail, not looking back to see if she was watching him go. He felt he had no heart left. Felt as if all he had in his life was being drained away from him, leaving him lonely and helpless, an unwanted wanderer. But this time he wouldn't go back. Not where he wasn't wanted. She'd got all she wanted from him, and now she didn't want to be bothered, so she'd simply seized on the first excuse to get rid of him.

At the Webster home Sylvia went on with her cleaning. There was no expression on her face. She didn't even look after him from the window.

* * *

He reached the road to Midvale just as the tail end of a bus was vanishing from sight over a dip. He knew the next one would be some time. He waited.

He couldn't take the chance of going back to where he'd come from.

A heavy lorry came croaking over the rise and towards him. He got up and thumbed it.

The driver slowed down and waited for him to hop in with his case. The lorry geared up again and he settled down, staring fixedly along the road ahead.

He was trying not to think — but

Sylvia kept crowding back into his mind, pushing all other thoughts aside. He lit a cigarette moodily and flicked the match towards the window. It was closed; the match fell on the floor. The driver, who had not spoken until then, yelped: 'Hey, watch what you're doin', bub!'

Eddie ground his foot on the match and grunted: 'Name's Eddie.'

'Mine's Joe. Glad to know you.'

Eddie sank back into his reverie.

The driver said: 'Got something on your mind?'

'Plenty.'

'You got somethin' on your *lips*, too, Eddie,' he grinned.

Eddie took a look in the left-hand driving mirror. He found his handkerchief and wiped away the lipstick smear. The driver chuckled. 'Dame trouble, huh?'

'That's it. Dame trouble.'

'They're a cuss,' said the driver. 'I know — I had plenty of experience. Takes a dame to make you forget a dame. That's what you need.'

'It could be.'

'There's a leetle red-headed number I

know in Midvale. If you like I'll fix it for you. She'll take your mind off whatever's on it. What say?'

Eddie said: 'I guess not. I'd be making comparisons.'

The driver said: 'Some dame, is she? Leavin' her?'

'What does it look like?'

'Wife? No? I thought not. Had a bust-up?'

'I blew my top and walked out.'

The driver said: 'Then why not walk in again? If she's as good as — '

Eddie growled: 'F'Christ's sake shut up about it!'

'Okay. Don't get so touchy.'

They rattled along another few miles. Eddie's face grew longer and longer. He felt in his pocket for his cigarettes and found a butt-end. He dragged it out — there was lipstick around the end. One of Sylvia's. He threw it fiercely on to the floor and ground it underfoot.

They rattled along another few miles. The driver murmured: 'Only twenty to Midvale. If you want me to fix you up with — '

Eddie grated: 'I don't. Stop the truck! I'll get out here!'

'Are you nuts? You're twenty miles from noplace here.'

'I said stop the truck! I get off here! I'll flag a lift back!'

* * *

It was almost two o'clock before he got back. She was out on the porch, watching the road. He came trudging along it, his bag a dead weight in his hand. His recently broken leg was beginning to tell on him, too.

He tramped in past her, without a word. He carried his case up to his room, then came down again.

'I've come back.'

'I knew you would. You can't break away, Eddie.' She had lost her iciness of the morning.

He said: 'I can't, I know that now. But it didn't seem to worry you much. You didn't try to persuade me to stay.'

She said: 'I felt you needed a lesson. I thought it best for you to see for yourself.

How far did you get?'

'I didn't even get to Midvale.'

'Poor Eddie. You *are* in a mess, aren't you?'

'How about Alex,' he demanded, ignoring the taunt. 'What did you tell him?'

'I didn't tell him anything. He's been worried about Annie today, too. She had a much stronger hold over him than even she knew. I believe that if she'd told him what she saw last night, and chanced his anger, he might really have believed her.'

'Then it's a good job for you she didn't.'

'And for you.'

Eddie took off his overcoat and pegged it.

'You must be tired and hungry, Eddie. I saved some lunch for you. It's in the kitchen.'

He followed her through and sat down to lunch. At length he said: 'I will say this in your favor — you're quite a cook.'

'I learned to cook long before I ever knew Alex as anything but the man who came around when Mother or Dad or any of my sisters were ill. It's like swimming or horse riding — once learned, never forgotten.'

He cleaned his plate. She leaned over him, her arms round his neck. Her perfume tantalized him.

She murmured: 'I'm glad you came back. I admit I couldn't face the prospect of being alone here with Alex, without anything to relieve the monotony. He's such a feeble lover — you can imagine.'

'I can — but I'd rather not. I don't like the idea of anyone else having the right — when I haven't. Why don't you take a chance and skip out with me?'

'Forget it, Eddie. Things are better now than they ever were, now Annie's gone. You see that?'

'But you aren't any closer getting to a city, like you want to. You never will, if Alex can help it.'

'Perhaps a time will come when he can't help it.'

Eddie looked uneasy. 'How d'you mean? When he's retired?'

'Perhaps. I spoke to him about going, today. Said why didn't we go and take you along with us as chauffeur. But he simply laughed and told me not to be so silly.'

'There you are. That's what he'll always do.'

She murmured: 'I can be patient — as long as we stay together.'

Between them they cleared the dishes quickly. He said: 'Where's Alex? Out?'

'He's taking a nap upstairs. He was worn out after last night.'

He nodded and said: 'When — when's he likely to be out for a while?'

'Soon. Miss Pinder, the school teacher down in the village, is expecting a baby.'

Eddie grinned. 'You mean *Mrs.* Pinder?'

'No, it's *Miss* Pinder. Quite a straight-laced young female, too. It's a nine days wonder down there. The authorities have given her notice.'

He said: 'Who's the lucky poppa?'

'So far, the gossips don't know. But they've accused almost every man in the village, including Alex. He's rather amused about it.'

Eddie said: 'Considering Garwood's just a backwood spot, with a few local yokels, plenty seems to happen there.'

'Plenty happens everywhere. But in a big town it doesn't get round. In a place like Garwood it does. If they didn't have things like that to gossip over they'd go mad through the dreariness of life as they know it.'

'It's a good job they don't know what's happening up here,' he reflected. 'That *would* give them something to talk about.'

★　★　★

Things drifted along quietly for the following two weeks. Doc Webster was out on his rounds most mornings, and at those times when Eddie didn't have to drive him they made the most of their time together. It was almost as if they were husband and wife, except for the doctor, and he seemed so inconspicuous that Eddie began to look on him almost as a lodger.

Nothing more was heard of, or from, Annie. The Sheriff paid a visit, and this time Eddie, behind the barrier of his new-grown moustache, faced him calmly if not very volubly. Sylvia noted that fact with amusement.

Thanksgiving Day and Christmas came and went. They saw the new year in together, the three of them.

Miss Pinder's baby came, and Miss Pinder went. The village got over it. Stopped trying to guess the father. The father, whoever he was, held his silence.

February found things going smoothly. Doctor Webster had no idea of the game that was being played on him. Sylvia had resigned herself to doing the work about the house. Eddie made himself as useful as he could, and the doctor privately congratulated himself on having Eddie around. Now that Annie was gone, he was a great help.

By the end of March the days were warm and sunny, and long before April drew to a close Garwood was basking in summer heat again.

Eddie's infatuation with Sylvia burned more fiercely than ever. Her voluptuousness never paled on him. Sylvia remained much the same. She never mentioned her feelings where he was concerned. He still did not know if she cared more or less for him — or even if she cared at all.

The hot summer blazed in, and Eddie remembered how, just under a year ago, he had trudged along the winding road to Garwood: a hunted man, running from the consequences of — he always stopped before thinking of *there*. Forced the affair from his conscience.

Under his willing hands the garden took shape. Tree roses formed a little arbor, sheltered from the casual glance at the bottom of the small lawn. He took special pride in it, and when the doctor was out he and Sylvia would often sit there, making love and listening for the sound of the doctor's car returning. When they heard it purring up the trail, Sylvia would run back to the kitchen and Eddie would grab a pair of shears or a spade and be working hard. They grew careless; their continued success in deluding Doctor Webster wiped away their previous caution.

There was only one thing to mar Eddie's satisfaction. That was his blind anger at such times as Webster spent the night with his wife, in her room. It required all Sylvia's persuasiveness to stop Eddie flying off the handle. He pleaded with her to leave with him, promised her he'd make money, begged her to run out on Alex. He was jealously possessive of another man's property.

She argued with him about it. 'I'm not going without knowing what I'm going *to*, Eddie. If you had something to offer I wouldn't hesitate — I don't like Alex mauling me, any more than you do. But he's providing for us both — can't you be content with what we have now? Maybe, sometime, things'll alter, and then . . . '

'How will they? I'm never likely to inherit a fortune. Nor to make one, hanging round here.'

They were in the rose arbor he had built. Alex had gone off in the car. Sylvia read the discontent in Eddie's eyes. She pulled his head forward and pressed her lips to his brow.

'You won't go now, Eddie. You can't. Less than ever now. Kiss me.

His lips came down to hers, and his

arms wound about her waist.

Suddenly everything was very quiet . . .

★ ★ ★

Alexander Webster cursed and surveyed the stationary car with an aggravated expression. The front wheel was lodged in a ditch at the bottom of the hill trail. The offside rear wheel was stuck in the air.

He got back into the car and started the engine. The motor hummed, but the car merely dug deeper into the ditch. He glanced about him. There was no one in sight to lend a hand. And he hadn't the strength to lift the car out of the rut alone. The house wasn't far — better walk back and get Eddie, he told himself. Eddie was young and strong. He would be able, with the doctor's help, to get the car righted again.

He reached the house, perspiring. The day was hot and the climb up, a stiff one. He went to the kitchen first to get himself a drink of water. He had expected to find Sylvia there, but she was not to be seen. Through the rear window he could see the garden and the rose arbor Eddie had planted, and which was already in bloom. Through the thick foliage about it he thought he caught a glimpse of some white garment.

Most likely Eddie in shirt sleeves, working on his pet project. He went through into the garden and trod over the lawn towards the rose arbor.

Sylvia lay back languidly, her green eyes staring past Eddie's shoulder at the sky. He stirred, breathing heavily. She said: 'We *do* have fun, don't we? All the time.'

He caressed her gently. 'Not exactly *fun*,' he murmured. 'It's more serious than that — to me, at least.'

'*And* to me, Eddie. Poor old Alex — if he had any idea . . . '

They were silent again whilst she lay submissive under his soft caressing. She yawned.

The voice came from outside the arbor — but almost on top of them! It was Alex, saying: 'Are you in there, Eddie . . . the car hit the ditch. I wondered — '

And whilst Eddie was still too shocked to make a move, Sylvia screamed: 'Alex

— Alex, help!' And then she was pushing and clawing at Eddie's face and body as Alex stepped into the arbor and stood petrified. 'Help me, Alex!' she sobbed. 'Oh, thank God you came back now! Get this beast away from me!'

Eddie was stunned. He didn't realize her purpose properly until Webster gripped his shoulder and pulled him savagely to his feet. Webster's face was dark. He snapped: 'What — what *is* this?'

Sylvia adjusted her dress, sobbing: 'Oh, Alex! I came out to ask him to cut a few roses for the table. I sat down to chat to him whilst he cut them, and then — he must have lost his self-control or something — you can see . . . Heaven knows what would have happened if you hadn't been here . . . Alex — !'

Eddie was standing there with a bitter twist to his lips. Doc Webster said: 'Is — is it true, Eddie?'

Eddie shrugged. 'Can you believe her?'

Webster muttered: 'I'm not going to waste any time recriminating you. Perhaps I can understand how you may have felt about Sylvia all this time. You should

244

be handed over to the sheriff — but I don't wish Sylvia to be involved in anything like that. You'd better go. Get packed and go at once, before I change my mind!'

11

Eddie packed again. That didn't take him long. He had bought a few things whilst he had worked for the doctor, but no more than would fit in the old case he had. He also counted the money he had saved — eighty-eight dollars exactly.

When he got downstairs he could hear Sylvia in the living room with the doctor. She was saying: 'Perhaps he didn't mean it — couldn't help it, Alex. He hasn't ever behaved like that before. Couldn't — couldn't you give him another chance?'

Eddie smiled, twistedly.

Webster said: 'No, my dear. I can make allowances for Eddie. I know he hasn't been near the village much, hasn't even spoken to a woman other than yourself and Annie since he came here, but I've no use for a man who can't control himself. In any case, if he feels that way about you it's better for him to go away. He'll be all right. If I did the right thing I'd hand him over to the sheriff . . . but I won't go that far. But he must go. Suppose it happened while I was on a night call?' She didn't answer. He went on: 'You stay here. No need for you to see him again . . . I'll just see if he's ready.'

He came out into the hall. Eddie was by then at the door, opening it. Webster said: 'I really am sorry about this, Eddie. I had no idea — '

Eddie grunted: 'Forget it, Doc. I asked for it. And thanks for all you've done for me.'

He walked out, closing the door, and Webster followed him.

At the gate, Webster said, awkwardly: 'Wait a minute, Eddie. I was wondering how you're placed for — money?'

'I've got some I saved. Eighty bucks.'

To his astonishment, the Doctor thrust a folded wad of dollar bills into his hand. 'There's another fifty. But I want you to get right away from Garwood, you understand? I don't want any talking done there. You know how they gossip. They may begin to add things together and wonder how it was you came to leave here. I want you to get right away . . . '

'I'll promise you that.' Sheepishly, Eddie put the money in his pocket. He started walking, got through the gates, and then turned again. 'Doc, you're a mug. But a swell mug.' Eddie ventured no further explanation. He began to walk down the trail, carrying the heavy case. Puzzled, Webster stood and watched until he was out of sight, then turned into the house again. He went into the library. Sylvia was by the window.

Webster shook his head. 'He seems genuinely sorry . . . perhaps I should have let him stay — given him another chance.'

Sylvia said swiftly: 'No, Alex. On thinking it over, you did right. I feel safer now he's gone. If he forgot himself once, he might have done so again. And you know I can't stand any man near me but you.'

He put his arm about her and said: 'If you're glad he's gone, that's all that matters. He won't dare come back here again.' He paused, then went on: 'It means you won't be able to go to town again, darling. Unless I can manage to find an odd night or so.'

'I haven't been for ages, anyhow. Not all the winter. Alex, why *don't* we move? You've worked here for thirty years now. Well, almost. It's time you saw a bit of life . . . let me show it to you, dear.'

He smiled. 'All the life I need is right here with these people — and with you! In a city life can be a very ugly thing at times. You wouldn't like it. It wouldn't fit in with your nature.'

She pouted like a child. 'But Alex — '

'No, dear. Apart from the difficulties of starting a new practice — and I'm far too old to start again now — there are other snags.'

She pleaded: 'You needn't work at all. You've enough saved for us both to retire on.'

He took her shoulders and looked at her tenderly. 'Sylvia, I'm not going to live forever. Even if I live my allotted span, you'll only be a middle-aged woman when I die. That's why I won't retire. I want to leave enough for you to live comfortably on when I'm not with you anymore.'

She shuddered. 'Please don't talk like that, Alex.'

'But you must face it, Sylvia. I haven't impressed it on you before, but — I have mentioned I suffer a little from heart trouble, I think. That's why I don't go dancing late with you, although I'd like to. But actually my heart is in far worse condition than I tell you. I may not live very long.'

She gasped: 'Alex — what do you mean?'

He thought the strange light in her green eyes was alarm. He said: 'Oh, don't worry yet. I may live fifteen years — certainly twelve.'

'Surely that's another reason why you should retire?'

'It wouldn't make so much difference, dear. It wouldn't stop the disease. And I must go on working. I can't be satisfied until I've saved a hundred thousand dollars. That's the figure I set myself when we married. That's the figure I mean to attain. Then you can ask me again.'

'But it'll take you *years* to save that much money!'

He sank into a chair. 'Then try and be patient, Sylvia. It's for you.' He rose suddenly. 'I forgot the car! It's fast in the ditch. Have to go into the village to get a lift . . . '

She watched him walking down the path from the window. Her lips were a tight line, her hands clenched on the sill. Under her breath she muttered: 'You bloody fool!'

★   ★   ★

The car was on the road again, on its four wheels. Webster halted in surprise. No one was about, as far as he could see. He got inside and saw the white paper that had been slipped under the release grip of the brake handle.

Thanks again, Doc, for everything. Eddie.

He sat staring at it for some time, then slid it into his pocket and started the car. He drove down the hill and through the village and onto the road leading down to the main highway.

He braked after a time and looked

down. Far beneath could be seen a solitary, plodding figure, laden with a case.

Satisfied Eddie really was going, and wasn't going to hang about, he turned the car and started his calls.

★ ★ ★

Eddie walked steadily on, with set lips. He had exerted himself to lift the car from the ditch, so much so that the strain had told on his recently healed leg. It ached fiendishly now.

He was almost glad of what had happened. He was well rid of her. He tried to persuade himself that it was only her sex that appealed to him. But it wouldn't work. He knew there was something else in both of them, but he didn't know what. Some impelling force, which held him against his will, made him a party to her desires and deeds, even though an unwilling one.

He shrugged and stepped more purposefully, ignoring his leg. He reached the main highway and sat down to wait for a bus or passing truck.

He swore to himself that this was to be the end. It had to be the end . . .

★   ★   ★

That night he lay on a cheap bed in the equally cheap Lord Nelson Hotel. He had reached the hotel — it being the only place he felt he could find some privacy — late that afternoon. By a stroke of chance he had been given the room Sylvia had occupied that night they had stayed in town so many months ago.

He had felt too dispirited to ask for another one. He lay on the bed, and he was dry-eyed and dry-mouthed; he didn't go out to eat, and he hadn't bothered to light the cigarettes he had with him. His fists were knotted under his head and he lay on his stomach and allowed the thoughts that were in his mind and heart to have their way with him.

His mood of satisfaction at the chance to get out without being able to run back to her, had vanished with the passing day. Now he knew only that he wanted her enough to do anything for her, to face anything for her.

Outside, the lamp standards flashed into life and cast eerie patterns across the window-side of the ceiling. The sounds of moving traffic reached the room faintly, as if they came from another world in which he had no part. Through the walls he could distinguish the continual mutter and mumble of two people talking in the next room. Every few minutes a woman's laugh sounded.

The night wore on and the sounds of traffic died away, and the couple next door stopped talking; only the lamplight on the ceiling remained to show that the world was alive. Beneath it, in the thick darkness, Eddie lay awake still. The darkness began to crawl away before the fingers of the dawn.

Eddie got up and felt his chin. Then he unstrapped his case and took from it his razor. He went to the washbowl and tried the hot faucet. After a few minutes, warm water came through. He filled the bowl and wet his beard, then plastered cream on his chin. He caught sight of his eyes in the mirror. Beneath each was a dark ring.

He flicked open the razor, then stopped suddenly, staring at the blade. His fingers trembled slightly as he raised it.

No! He was too much of a coward for that. It took a brave or a desperate man to kill himself. He rinsed the razor and washed, then cleaned his teeth. His clothes were dusty, and lacking a brush he dusted them off with his hands.

It had been a miserable night. But it was over. He had over one hundred and thirty dollars in hard cash. That was something. Wisely used, it could be a lot of help in making him forget.

He went back to the bed and lay on it, waiting for the morning. The wash and shave had altered things in some way. He no longer felt like a condemned man. He would go out now and eat; then he would take the town in, being careful not to make himself too conspicuous. Later he would eat again and perhaps take in a movie. Then, at night, he would have a few drinks and go along to some dance hall, where he might be able to find some distraction.

He followed his plans closely. He ate and did the town; he ate again and saw a movie, then he drank Scotch whisky and went along to the local 'Jive Joint'. But the women there were just teenagers; compared to them he felt like an old man. They were happy; had no troubles and no past. He knew at once he didn't fit in, and the blare of the band drove him out into the night again after a few minutes.

A woman smiled at him by the corner. She wore short skirts and a tight blouse. A cheap fur was wound about her throat, and a cheap brooch glittered at the neck of her blouse. She spoke to him. 'Stranger to town, Mister?'

He mumbled something and hurried on. He realized suddenly that this night was not going to be any different from the night before; it was, if anything, going to be worse. His whole being cried out for the sight and touch of Sylvia. He hopped a bus just outside town and made his silent way through the darkness towards Garwood.

He went through the woods past the pool, where he stood a moment, giving way to nostalgic memories. He kept to the trees and made his way towards the rear of the Webster home. There was a light in the kitchen window — and he could see Sylvia drying dishes! His heart jumped, he forgot caution and hurried forward, past the rose arbor he had made, over the tiny lawn —

Another figure came into view. It was Webster, wearing a ridiculous little apron, and laughing. He was drying his hands. He had obviously been washing whilst Sylvia dried. As Eddie stared, he kissed Sylvia lightly on the neck, then they both went out, switching off the light.

Wild, impossible thoughts crowded Eddie's mind as he stood there. If he waited, waited until they'd gone to bed, then took the ladder and tried to attract Sylvia's attention . . . if she let him in . . . if they kept very quiet and she locked her door . . .

He realized how foolish he was being. Sylvia might not want to let him in. Webster might report him if he caught him.

But unable to help himself, he stayed;

he crept round to the front of the house and found a refuge in a clump of shrubbery. He waited.

The library light went off at about eleven. A light appeared in Sylvia's window. Eddie felt his body tauten with desire. Was his idea of getting the ladder so mad? Maybe she would let him in!

He sneaked back to the shed for the ladder, then cursed when he found the door padlocked.

Back to the front. Perhaps Webster would be called out. If he was, Eddie decided he could take the chance of knocking and getting Sylvia down to let him in. His leg ached abominably, and his body was weary through lack of sleep. Several times he felt himself dozing off where he crouched, and at last his head drooped and he slept, leaning against the thick branch of the dwarf bush behind him.

The light went out in Sylvia's room, and the entire house was quiet.

The fluting of birds in the trees along the hill road brought Eddie to wakefulness again. The sun had risen; he judged the time to be about eight o'clock.

Now, if he waited — Webster would be going out on his calls, and then he would be able to see Sylvia!

He ran a comb through his hair and settled down to wait another hour. There were signs of life in the house. Webster himself came out and went to the shed for wood. Smoke rose from the kitchen stove-stack.

Sylvia came to the door for a moment, went to the mailbox at the gate, unlocked it and took out the delivery. She passed within ten yards of Eddie, but he refrained from making his presence known. Best to wait until Webster had gone.

After what seemed a hundred years to Eddie, the doctor came out. He was whistling cheerfully as he unlocked the garage and went in to the car. Eddie listened to the motor purring. The bonnet poked carefully into the drive, followed by the rest of the car. Webster stepped out at the door and shouted: 'Ready, darling?'

Sylvia came out, wearing a hat and coat. The coat pulled tight against her taut little figure, and Eddie found his body aching for her. She said: 'All ready, Alex. You can drop me at the general store, then I'll do my shopping. Pick me up at the snack bar when you're through with your calls, dear.'

She stepped into the car and they drove off. Eddie cursed aloud. Of course! Now *she* had to attend to the shopping. He wasn't there to get things for her, nor was Annie.

He got up and cut through into the woods. He felt a lot better now. It had done him good just to see her, to know she was there, to be able to feel that he could reach her at any time if he had to. Perhaps he would come and wait tomorrow night . . . Or maybe he could contact her by letter. If he let her know where he was staying, she might get in touch with him.

Of course she wasn't gone from his life. She was still there. And if he gave her a few weeks alone with Alex, without even Annie to relieve the boredom of life, she might change her mind about money being more important to her than the love he could offer her.

He felt quite light-hearted as he tramped back towards the road to Midvale.

* * *

But Eddie's lightness of heart didn't last.

With the onset of the night again came that aching, irrepressible misery. He wanted her near to him.

He haunted the bars in the neighborhood of the Lord Nelson and made a start on getting rid of his money. After closing time he wandered about the streets, thinking. Perhaps Webster *would* be called out that very night. It would be just his luck to miss the opportunity! He found his steps taking him in the direction of the bus stop.

No one was waiting. He found a timetable and studied it by the aid of a match. The last bus had gone half an hour earlier. He gave a grunt of disappointment and started the walk back to his hotel.

The night clerk was on duty. As Eddie

took the key he said: 'I've got a note for you, Mister Martin.'

'A note?' It was hard to keep the tremendous excitement he felt out of his voice.

The clerk threw it over. 'Lady dropped in about two hours ago. Wanted to know if a Mister Martin was staying here. When she found you were out she wrote this and left it with me. Gave me a buck.'

Eddie took the mauve envelope eagerly. 'Thanks. Here's another buck to go with the other.'

He almost ran up the stairs to his room. He could scarcely wait to close the door. He flicked on the light and ripped open the envelope, breathing quickly.

Darling Eddie,

I want to see you. Things are so horribly dull here without you. I must see you! I can't take any chances like coming here again — but if you're not doing anything tomorrow, midday, I'll tell you where we can meet in safety.

There's a movie house in Midvale called the 'Universal News Theatre'.

It's on Old Elm Street, on the corner. At midday it's nearly always empty because the show's just started. If you go in the twenty-cent seats through the third door on the left in the foyer, you'll find me on the back row of the aisle opposite that door, on the left-hand side.

I don't know if you wish to see me, dear, not after the trick I played on you with Alex. But I had to do that, Eddie; you know why.

Anyway, I'll be there — please come. I've been so sad since you went away . . .

Do I need to say I love you, Eddie? Your S

He held the letter in his hands for a long time. There was a damp spot near the signature, almost as if a teardrop had fallen there. But he hardly thought she felt that badly. He wouldn't have been surprised if she'd planted that wet spot herself for effect, and to make sure he'd keep the date.

Well, she needn't have gone to *that*

trouble. He'd keep the date quick enough without any stage effects. He placed the letter under the pillow; that night he slept more peacefully than he had for a long time.

★   ★   ★

The attendant said: 'First door on the right, sir.'

'It's all right, thanks. I'm meeting a friend inside.'

The foyer clock said twelve-oh-one. Eddie counted the doors very carefully and found the one he wanted.

Inside the News Theatre it was dark. There was an old Donald Duck cartoon on. He could tell by the hollow sound of the laughter that there were few people in the theatre. He located the head of the aisle facing him. The seats on the left side were empty. He paused, then looked to the right. There were two people there, man and woman. They were middle-aged. There was no one else in the immediate vicinity.

On the screen, Donald Duck was

getting involved with the mainspring of a tower clock. Eddie dropped into the first seat. Goofy was being hammered about inside a large bell by two metal figures that chimed the hour.

He waited, hardly seeing the screen. The cartoon comedy ended and the newsreel came on. He didn't watch it. He wasn't interested in the great fire that had ravaged a hotel, costing over a hundred lives. Nor was he interested in Joe Louis's new bar. He sat through a short comedy and another Walt Disney, a silly symphony. The green illumination on the face of the clock at the back of the theatre told him the time was now twelve-eighteen.

He didn't go; there was still a chance of her coming. The lights went up and a trailer was shown. Then an advertising subject. Then the lights dimmed and another cartoon was shown. He read the title listlessly: 'The Clock Cleaners'. He received a shock when he saw it was the feature that had been showing on his arrival. He waited until it ended, then rose to leave. And a woman said: 'Excuse me, please.'

'*Sylvia* — '

'Shhh! Not so loud, Eddie.'

She went past him to the second seat and sat down.

He hissed: 'It's turned one. Where the devil have you been?'

'Sorry, dear. I couldn't get away — I hoped I'd be able to slip out the minute Alex started his calls, but he was late going. I had to wait and that made me miss the bus. I'm sorry if you've had a long wait.'

'It's all right, as long as you're here now.' He felt her shoulder against his and smelled the fragrance of her perfume. His arm went about her shoulder; he leaned sideways and kissed her, hard and long.

'That was nice . . . Listen, Eddie. I'm sorry about having to tell Alex you attacked me. Can you ever forgive me for that?'

He said shortly: 'Don't mention it again. It's forgiven. I can't get along without you, Sylvia. I want you to stay with me, now. Let's clear out of Midvale and start a new life somewhere, together.'

She murmured against his ear: 'Even if

we could — even if I was willing — we wouldn't get away with it. You're a fool, Eddie. You must know Alex would go right to the police if I vanished now. He'd be sure to suspect you had a hand in it. Then they'd trace us. They'd look for us all over the country.'

He was silent a moment; her cool hand found his.

'I've got a better idea, Eddie. If you help me, we can have our life together — and seventy thousand dollars!'

He stiffened. 'What are you talking about, Sylvia? How is that possible?'

'Alex, Eddie. We must murder Alex!'

Eddie gasped aloud with shock.

'Don't say anything until you've heard what I have to say,' she added quickly. 'And don't sound so shocked.'

'You can't do it, and I won't help you,' he said flatly. 'Even *you* can't do that!'

'Think what it means — and there wouldn't be any danger. It'd be easy. It's been in my mind now for the last two days. Since the night you left. I didn't know where to find you at first; then I remembered that the only quiet hotel you knew in Midvale was the Lord Nelson. That's why I borrowed the car — I told Alex I was going over to see a relative of mine. He wasn't too keen, but when I promised I'd be home early, he said it was all right. As it turned out, you *had* stayed at the Lord Nelson.'

'How did you know I'd stay in Midvale at all?' he asked.

Softly she said: 'I knew, Eddie.'

'But you can't murder Alex,' he whispered hoarsely. 'It wouldn't be human. Schaparelli was different, though even that was bad enough. But your own husband — who's treated you decently — '

'It's his own fault,' she muttered. 'If he hadn't sent you away I'd never have thought of doing it. And he utterly refuses to move to a big city. I can't *stand* Garwood anymore. I'm through. I want to go away with you, Eddie.'

'Then let's go — but leave Alex his life, at least.'

She said, in an altered voice: 'Why should *you* be so afraid of murder? When you're a killer yourself!'

12

Eddie took it more calmly than she had expected. She felt the arm that was about her stiffen, but apart from that he did not betray his feelings either in action or in tone of voice.

'What do you mean?'

She half sneered: 'Don't give me the innocent act, Eddie. You came to Garwood running away from something. You took Alex in by some silly story about stealing a few dollars. But you didn't take *me* in. For one thing, I repaired your jacket that was torn, and I saw that, apart from the fact that the jacket was dusty and rumpled, it was a comparatively new one. That argued that you hadn't been on the road long. That started my suspicions. I noted the fact that the tag inside said 'Levenheim, New York City'. That was the tailor's mark. That told me you came from New York. All the way to Garwood! I looked up a sales catalogue and found

Levenheim — they're one of the classiest tailors in New York.'

Eddie muttered: 'That proves nothing.'

'No, it doesn't. But I began to wonder why an obviously well-to-do man from New York would run up here suddenly and try to lose himself. I knew it must be something big, and I asked the sheriff of Garwood to pass over his police 'wanted' circulars . . . '

Eddie hissed: 'You *what?* You *fool* — !'

'You needn't worry. He doesn't suspect. He thinks it's just that I'm interested in criminology.'

Eddie murmured: 'Not so loud! Go on.'

'I found a photograph of *you* in that circular. It mentioned that Eddie Kark of New York was wanted urgently on a charge of murder.'

'My name's Martin.'

'Really, Eddie! I heard that man call you Kark that night at the Hole In The Wall Club. So why deny it? I won't give you away, trust me.'

He saw the futility of argument. He grunted: 'All right. I'm Kark. But just

270

because I am doesn't mean I'm a killer. Just because of some damn crazy story about first degree murder, it doesn't say I'd kill again.'

'You aren't going to tell me you were framed?' she smiled.

'No, I killed that man all right. But not intentionally. His name was Joslin. Medcalf Joslin. I doubt if that was his original name, but that was the name I knew him under. I met him in the Skyline Club soon after my return from the forces. He was introduced to me by a casual acquaintance of mine.

'I liked him. He was young, and he had a friendly way with him. He had a really dry sort of humor. Any man who can make me laugh wins all my confidence. I can't envisage a rotten crook being so witty and seeming so straightforward. Joslin was both. He could look you in the face and hail as you as a comrade, while underneath he was scheming against you.

'I had about ten thousand dollars saved. It had taken me a long time to save it. Before, during, and after the war. I was looking around, thinking of buying myself a junior partnership in some up-and-coming firm. I hadn't been dead straight before the war; but I wanted to change all that. Joslin offered me a chance to double my money. He explained his plans for starting a new firm of magazine productions. He painted a very pretty picture. He showed me figures to prove there was a wide market for the type of mags he meant to turn out.

'I liked the notion of being a publisher. I pictured myself inside a few months sitting in a comfortable office chair with a stenographer on my knee, refusing to see struggling writers. I was going to be a big shot. Eventually I might even buy out Hearst! Eddie Kark, power publisher!'

He paused, and laughed softly and bitterly. 'I acted like a prize hick from Indiana. Without anything other than a gentleman's agreement, I handed over my money to Joslin. The idea was for him to lease offices, get things rolling. I was to walk in as junior partner and director when the offices had been attended to. But once I'd handed over the money, somehow I didn't seem to see much of

Joslin anymore. I put it down to the fact that he was busy attending to details, and let things go.

'After about a month I started to get suspicious that he was deliberately avoiding me. I'd had no reply to my letters. So I phoned. He answered all right. He said there was trouble about the office, and he was having a tremendous job to locate a suitable spot. I let things go for another month.

'I only realized then what I'd done. I'd given every dollar I had, almost, to someone who was virtually a stranger to me! I hadn't a line in writing, hadn't a solitary witness to show I'd handed him the money. Even more, I hadn't paid him by cheque, at his own request. He'd claimed he wanted the cash to commence negotiations, and wanted it to start an immediate account with. Twenty thousand of his and ten of mine. That was why he hadn't answered my letters — he didn't care to put anything into writing that I might use against him if he was swindling me.

'I felt good and mad. I phoned him

again — asked how he was spending the money. He seemed not to know who I was. He disclaimed any knowledge of my money, denied having taken a cent from me. He asked me what kind of game *I* was trying to pull on *him*!

'I was madder than I'd ever been. I almost lost my mind. I slammed down the receiver, rooted through my trunks and found an army revolver I'd bought during my overseas service. I loaded it and slid it into my pocket.

'I didn't intend to kill him! I just wanted to frighten him, I swear that. I wanted to point the gun at him and force a confession from him. I wanted to either get a written agreement or my money back.

'That night, when I walked up the stairs to his flat, there was no thought of murder in my mind. I didn't go by stealth. I went quite openly. I'd been to see him there before. The janitor knew me, and saw me, on my way up. He said good evening to me. I asked him if Joslin was home.

'The desk clerk saw me, too. But since

I wasn't going up there to do anything other than try and recover my money, I didn't worry about them, and hardly gave the matter a thought.

'Joslin was in. He was entertaining a woman. When I walked in he told her to wait in the other room. She went out and closed the door after her. Joslin lay on the settee, smoking, in his dressing gown, his feet in slippers. He seemed as cool as I was wild.

' "Well?' he said coldly. 'What's the big idea of busting in on a private little party like this? Don't you ever knock?'

' "I'm going to knock — ' I told him grimly. 'I'm going to knock you to Kingdom Come unless I get satisfaction from you. How about it?'

' "How about what?' he demanded. 'And before you start any rough stuff, may I remind you of the penalty for assault and — '

' "I'm not worrying about that. It'll be worth it. And it isn't assault and battery I'm going for, either. It's murder!'

'I got the gun from my pocket smoothly enough, and I thought I saw

275

him start momentarily. He claimed to know nothing about my money. He admitted having been introduced to me, but accused me of lying and extortion.

'I pointed the gun at him. I grated: 'Joslin, unless you hand me back my roll within ten seconds — I'll shoot, I swear it!'

'I managed to look the part. I saw a trace of fear come into his eyes for the first time. But he still stuck to his story.

'So I began to count: 'One — two — three — '

'He was uneasy by now. He said: 'I don't keep that much money on the premises, anyway. I — '

''Four — five — six — '

'My hand was steady on the gun. With my thumb I slid the safety catch off.

''*Seven* — '

''All I have here is five hundred,' he said hurriedly. 'If I give you that now and you see me tomorrow — '

''Not a chance. By tomorrow you'll either have skipped or have hired someone to finish *me* off before I finish *you*! *Eight* — '

'He was panting now, and drops of sweat were on his face. I said:

' ''Nine . . . ' and let him see my finger tightening on the trigger slightly. He cried: 'Wait a minute! If you won't take it that way, how *can* I do anything about it?'

' ''Write down a confession. I can hold that until you pay me — or take it to court.'

'I could see him wavering. I must have relaxed a little, for he suddenly found courage and snarled: 'No, I'm *damned* if I will! You won't shoot — you daren't!'

'I wouldn't have shot, either, Sylvia. I knew right then I was licked. He'd read it in my eyes that I was pulling a big bluff. I don't know *what* would have happened then, because I never had the chance to find out. Just at that second, when I stood undecided, the trigger still tense under my finger, something happened to change everything.

'I'd forgotten the girl who'd been in the room when I'd arrived. I was standing with my back to the door she'd gone through — most likely a bedroom. But she hadn't forgotten *me*. She must have been afraid I meant what I said. She'd opened the door quietly — and at that very moment she chose to hurl a heavy vase across the room at me!

'She was a good aim. It struck me in the small of the back . . . I pitched forward, my finger involuntarily tightening the last few fractions of an inch . . . the gun exploded loudly . . . I recovered my balance . . .

'Joslin was slowly rolling from the settee. Between his eyes was an ugly black puncture. The girl screamed, whilst I stood paralyzed. I lost my head for a few minutes. I dropped the gun and ran across to the room where she was. She backed inside and tried to slam and lock the door. My foot burst it open before she turned the key. I jumped to the corner where she was crouching, hands in front of her. I sent a left for her jaw, and she collapsed with a gentle moan.

'I threw her onto the bed, turned and looked quickly at Joslin. He was good and dead. I was horrified about that. I realized too well what a jury would think.

'I was still standing there in a daze

when the outer door was flung open and someone called: 'Are you all right, Mister Joslin?'

'There wasn't much time to lose. I turned and ran back into the bedroom. I shut and locked the door behind me. I went to the window, ignoring the girl. I looked out for the fire escape. It was along at the next window, the window of the room I'd just left. I heard a startled shout from in there. Whoever it was had found the corpse. I had to move fast.

'There was the narrowest of ledges running along the wall. This was where my battle training was going to come in handy. I reached up and gripped it with my fingers. It was grooved on top and gave a good hold. I swung carefully out and started working along the wall. Down below, almost two hundred feet below, I could see the lights of lamp standards and crawling ears.

'Inch by inch, foot by foot, I edged along. I came to the escape. Then I was on it, and safe. I paused to take breath and to look through the window. I could see the janitor at the telephone. The desk clerk was standing in the doorway with a dazed expression. Joslin lay where I had left him, untouched. The bedroom door was still locked. The janitor put down the phone, looked up — and looked right at me. For a second his lips moved feebly. Then he yelled: 'There he is. There's the guy who killed him!'

'They started in a rush for the window, both of them. I ran down the escape, recklessly. The window shot up and they started shouting after me. About a hundred feet up there was a balcony leading all round the building. The upper escapes led to this, and round at the back one escape served the whole upper floors. I raced round the balcony, leaving the janitor and clerk yelling their heads off. I got down the escape, which terminated in a dark side street. I lost myself in the shadows, made my way to the main stem and just wandered.

'They put a net out for me, but I managed to elude it. I spent the night down by the docks, on an old wharf, underneath the shorings. No one came down there.

'I began to realize how things were going to look for me. I hadn't meant to kill — but the least I would be likely to get would be life. There were the facts that I had the gun ready for immediate shooting, and the woman had overheard me declare I meant to shoot him.

'It wasn't until then I remembered I'd left the gun back in the room. One more point of damning evidence against me. I knew it was no use facing it. I knew I wouldn't stand a chance. I didn't have the nerve to go back to my apartments, either. The cops would most likely have them under guard by that time. The only thing I could do was to get out of town.

'I got out. I thumbed my way by lorry and truck. I walked; I rode the rods. I got as far away as I could and still kept moving. I was sweating with fear. I was afraid of what they'd do to me if they got me. I was afraid of being third-degreed.

'By midday I was more than two hundred miles from New York. But it wasn't far enough. I bought a paper and read about myself. It was all there, photo as well, which some snoopy reporter had got from my rooms. It said clearly enough I was wanted on a count of murdering Joslin.

'So I kept on the move by rail and lorry, truck and coach. I skipped any big towns, bypassing them. I ate in back-street dumps, or at roadhouses. I slept out.

'Twelve days after I started running I reached Garwood. And the rest you know yourself.

'But I never intended to murder Joslin. Never even dreamed of it. It was an accident . . . ' He broke off, panting. She could feel his hand shivering against hers. She tightened her grip on it.

'So that's how it was, Eddie?'

'Just how it was. You believe me, Sylvia?'

She pressed his hand again. 'I do, darling. But — the police wouldn't, Eddie; if ever they get you they'll be certain to go all out for the death penalty! They'll say the whole thing was premeditated. And you *know* that — that's why you're running.'

The attendant came soft-footedly along

and shone a torch on them.

'Quiet there, please.'

Sylvia lowered her voice to a scarcely audible whisper.

'I won't give you away, Eddie — not if you do as I say with Alex! You've *got* to help me, Eddie. Otherwise — '

He rasped: 'You bitch, you wouldn't *dare*! I know too much about you!'

'Could you prove anything? No. There's no way out for you. It's one of two things: a prison cell, and later — execution, or seventy thousand dollars — and *me*! Make your choice now.'

He mumbled wretchedly: 'I couldn't!'

'All right then, Eddie. You'd better start getting away from town right now. I give you an hour — at the end of that hour I'll be waiting in the Fresco Café in Moon Avenue. If you haven't arrived to do as I say by then, I'll go straight to the police.' She stood up, leaned, and kissed his cheek lightly. 'That's just in case I don't see you again. I won't say goodbye — because I have a feeling I *will*. Seventy thousand dollars is a lot of money. A lot more than you've already killed one man for.'

He said: 'I don't want the money that badly.'

She said: 'Perhaps you don't. But don't forget, Eddie — I go with it!' She went, and he sat staring stupidly at the screen across which Donald Duck was still wrestling with a recalcitrant clock spring.

★ ★ ★

Sylvia tapped her foot impatiently and looked at her tiny wristwatch, her engagement present from Alex. It was a nice watch, studded with small diamonds, and had cost Alex a pretty penny. But he hadn't been quite so generous *after* their marriage. She failed to appreciate that he was saving for her. She preferred to spend it now whilst she was young. What good would seventy thousand dollars be to a grey-haired old crone?

She looked from the window of the Fresco along the dry, sun-baked street on the outskirts of the town. It was little more than a snack bar for motorists. She had chosen it because it was extremely unlikely anyone who knew her would see her there.

It was five minutes after the hour she had given Eddie. And she was starting to worry. Perhaps he wouldn't come! Perhaps she hadn't driven him *that* far.

She smiled suddenly. Here he was, his shoulders hunched, walking along the road towards the place. She knew what had brought him. It wasn't altogether the threat of the police — she hadn't intended to acquaint them with his identity, anyway. It was *herself* — the fascination she held for him.

He opened the door and stepped inside. The attendant said: 'What's for you, Mister?'

'Hamburger and coffee.'

'Comin' up.'

The place was empty but for the three of them. Eddie collected his order and brought it over, sitting down beside Sylvia.

'I knew you'd come!'

'One of these days maybe I won't.'

'If that ever happens it'll be because you won't be able.'

He said: 'I guess you're right. Well . . . '

'Wait a minute.' She got up, staring hard at the youth behind the counter who had been eyeing her silk-clad legs and listening to their conversation.

She failed to embarrass him. He said: 'They always *do* come, lady.'

'Suppose *you* mind your own hamburgers?'

'I would if I had some like you, lady! Oh boy!'

'You cute adolescent,' she sneered, and went over to the jukebox against the wall, plugging in a nickel. An undernourished voice filtered through, singing 'Temptation'. Sylvia returned to her seat and the fresh kid behind the lunch counter sniffed and resumed washing dishes, unable to hear anything more.

Sylvia said: 'You're agreeable to helping me?'

'I came here to try to talk you out of it. Get you to run away with me.'

'Then you may just as well get out now and I'll put that police call through. Will you help?'

He whispered: 'I — I guess so, but what if we're caught?'

Sylvia smiled triumphantly and leaned closer. 'Pull yourself together, Eddie. My plan's foolproof. It'll be put down as accidental death. Hit and run driver . . . '

'Hit and run — *driver?*' he gasped.

'Yes. Here's how we'll arrange it. Tomorrow night you'll be waiting here, on this road, at ten o'clock. At about eight I shall tell Alex I want to slip into the village to see some friends. He isn't expecting any night calls just now, and I'll borrow the car from him. I'll drive into the village, and see my friends. At nine o'clock I'll leave, ostensibly to drive home again.

'But I *won't* drive home. I'll drive down here and pick you up. Then we'll both run out to the center road that cuts right through the hill. It isn't much of a road, and it's banked by steep clay sides. It has no footpath. Cars don't usually use it. Before we do that we'll stop at a public telephone and I'll ring Alex — I'll tell him I'm Mrs. Casson who lives over the hill, and that my husband's in terrible agony with his stomach. Alex'll hurry right over. Old Casson has stomach ulcers, and he's a close friend of Alex's. If Alex thinks one of the ulcers has perforated the lining of the stomach he'll just grab his bag and rush out, so that if it has he'll he able to send for an ambulance without any loss of time.

'I'll have the car — therefore Alex will have to walk and take the quickest route, which is the center hill road. We'll reach it before him, and we'll stay at the top of the rise. When he starts walking up — and it's impossible for him to make a jump for safety, owing to the high sides of the road — we'll drive down at top speed. It's that simple. Then I'll drive home and say I've been there ever since I left the village, if anyone enquires.'

Eddie shuddered and said: 'I can't believe you could be so cold-blooded! You wouldn't do that — to Alex?'

Her mouth tightened. 'Alex is getting old — he's hidebound. And he's ruining my life. You don't know how I've hated living with him all this time, keeping up a pretense, acting like a giggling schoolgirl. The old fool deserves all he gets.'

He sent hot coffee coursing down his

throat. He seemed cold.

'It's *you* or *him*, Eddie. Which is it to be?'

Eddie said: '*Him*, of course.'

'That's better. You can't afford to be a sentimental idiot. It's not your nature, and even if it was you aren't in any position to act and feel like a good Samaritan.'

He put in: 'Since I'm almost forced into this, let me point out one or two flaws in the stunt. One: If you aren't back by eleven, Alex'll be worried and he'll go along to the village to find you. He'll find you left at about nine.'

'He won't. I won't say which of my friends I'm visiting. He won't ask. He's been doing a lot of studying in the library lately after dinner and forgets the time. And he won't leave the house without anyone there at night, in case there is a sudden call.'

Eddie nodded. 'Assuming that's as you claim, how about if he won't let you go?'

'I can coax him. If anything does happen to prevent me, don't wait after ten o'clock. If I'm not here by ten I'll come the night after. Do you understand?'

'I get that, but there's one other thing. The tires on the car! They'll leave tracks. If anyone happens to see they're the same type as the tires on Alex's own car, there's sure to be some awkward questions — '

'I'm not quite *insane*,' Sylvia told him. 'I told you I had it all mapped out. In the shed there's a set of old tires of a different make. They've been there six years and more, ever since Alex took them off the car ages ago. I think he's forgotten they're there himself. When I set out to meet you those tires will be loaded into the back of the rumble seat. I'll pick you up — we'll stop off in a quiet spot and change them for the tires on the car. We'll put the present tires into the rumble. Then we'll finish the — job. When it's over you'll change the tires back again.'

'And — how about the old tires?'

She reflected. 'I had thought of sinking them somewhere. But — we have to make sure of getting rid of those altogether. So I've thought of the best place to get rid of them. Out up on the hilltop, on the high, wild part of the crag which overhangs Garwood, there're a lot of natural caverns. Inside one of these is a natural pipeline . . . a funnel, running down into the heart of the hill itself. We used to have fun there when we were kids, tossing stones into it and trying to hear them drop at the bottom. We estimated its depth at more than five hundred feet. There was a geologist once who came to inspect it. He had himself lowered on a rope chair. He didn't manage to reach bottom. Since then — and that was fifteen years ago — it hasn't been touched. Kids here still go to play about the top of it, but they're harmless enough. That's where we'll pitch the tires, Eddie.'

'It *sounds* all right,' he murmured. 'Abut how about the width? Will the tires fit?'

'Easily. It's about four feet across, roughly circular. It keeps almost exactly that width for as far as you can see. They'll go down, Eddie. I know they will.'

He gazed at her suddenly. 'I don't like it.'

'Neither do I. But I'm not going to

have Alex round my neck any longer
— and I'm not going to miss the chance
of that money.'

'I believe you've been thinking up all
this for a long time!'

'Quite a long time — before I met you.
Since the day I married Alex, in fact. But
it wouldn't have come to anything if I
hadn't met you. You made me realize just
what I was missing — what I was capable
of with a man to do the heavy work.
Indirectly it's your own fault.'

Eddie said: 'I hope you change your
mind before tomorrow, Sylvia. But if you
don't — well, I'll change the tires and the
rest of it. But you'll have to handle the
wheel yourself. I couldn't do *that* to
Alex . . . '

She smiled. 'I planned to handle the
wheel, Eddie. I'm not forgetting how you
nearly made an awful mess of things that
night when we went to see Schaparelli.'

The jukebox had clicked off, and they
noticed the counter-hand was leaning
forward again. Eddie got up and said:
'Why don't you mind your own business,
Mister?'

'Sorry, friend. More coffee?'

'Sure, more coffee. And less curiosity.'

'Comin' up.'

Sylvia said: 'Plug another nickel in the box, Eddie. I feel like dancing.'

He plugged another nickel in. Crosby sang 'Black Moonlight'.

Sylvia got up and they danced slowly in the small, clear space between the tables. The counter-hand regarded them admiringly. He was wishing the dance was an 'excuse me'.

After a few minutes Sylvia said: 'There's a heavy truck pulling into the side. Maybe we'd better get out now, Eddie. I have to be getting back again. Alex will be in for lunch at two fifteen — and it's almost that now.'

He nodded and released her. His arms and body still tingled from the sensation her nearness gave him.

She said: 'I'll go first, dear. You wait a while.' She paused at the door. The counter-hand was busy. She said: 'Until tomorrow night, Eddie! Then we needn't ever part again!'

13

The car came hurtling down the long road in the gathering dusk. Fifty yards from the Fresco Café Eddie was sitting on a wooden fence at the roadside, waiting. It was nine-thirty. He hadn't expected her so soon. Evidently she was anxious to see if he would turn up for that fatal date after all.

She needn't have worried. Her last remark — after tomorrow they needn't ever part again, she'd said, or something like that — had deeply affected him. He was going through with it. He wanted her that badly.

Here was his chance to quit wandering. He felt he couldn't be happy *with* her — but he knew he couldn't even *live* without her.

She braked the car. He opened the door and stepped inside. She swung the car round and they shot along the road to Garwood. Halfway there she turned off onto a slightly narrower road.

For the first time she spoke: 'This takes us round the hill.'

Halfway down the road she drew up and pulled in to the side of the road. She offered him a cigarette. He took it and lit it. His hand was trembling violently. He noticed that hers was as steady as if she'd simply been out on a pleasurable picnic.

Almost accusingly, she said: 'You're jittery! I don't want you to go soft at the last minute.'

'I won't.'

She smoked her cigarette out and glanced at her wristwatch. 'Ten fifteen.' It was almost dark now. She went on: 'I think we can carry on. Better get along to the spot where we're changing the tires. They're in the back — the rumble seat.'

He kneaded his hands whilst she drove to the spot she had mentioned. They were very cold. But he was going through with it. It was too late to back out now.

They cut out onto another main road. Halfway along, the rough wooden fencing ceased and the road had a border of trees. She chose a convenient space and turned the car off into it. She cut the lights and stopped the motor.

'Now, Eddie. Hurry.'

He slid from the car and round to the rumble. She was there as quickly as him, the key already fitted. The rumble swung open and he hoisted the four decrepit tires from inside. 'The tools?'

'On the back seat.'

He got the tools, and found them icily cold in his already frozen fingers. Sylvia stood by and watched whilst he jacked up the car and started swinging the nut-brace. The movement warmed him. One by one the nuts were dropped to the ground. He slid the wheel away and got busy with the tire levers.

Sylvia looked continually at her watch. At length she took over the replacement of the wheels whilst Eddie carried on with the opposite ones.

At eleven-twenty they were ready to move again. The car tires were packed into the rumble, the tools laid away. Sylvia took the wheel and they swung onto the road. The headlights cut through the darkness. They cruised along slowly,

Sylvia keeping her eyes open for the phone booth.

When they reached it, she cut the lights again and they both got out to crowd into the cubicle. She slicked a nickel into the slot, dialed her own number, and got through to her husband.

'Webster home. Doctor Webster speaking.'

Sylvia raised the handkerchief she had ready, covered her lips with it and spoke into the mouthpiece.

'Doctor — this is Mrs. Casson — yes — Doctor, please come right over. Yes, my husband. His ulcers. He's in horrible pain. I don't know — yes, I'll do that until you get here. Please hurry. He's been like this for almost half an hour now.' She slammed the receiver down. Her face was twisted in a smile. 'Poor old Alex. He's quite upset about Casson. Told me what to do until he got there. He's starting out right now.'

They went out of the booth and got into the car again. She said: 'Now comes the important part, Eddie. Feel all right?'

'I feel bad about it. Why not change

your mind while there's still time?'

'Not now, Eddie. Not now!' Her hands gripped the wheel tightly. Her foot drove down on the gas. They roared along the road and came to a turn leading up on to the hilly territory. She turned and changed gears. They ground up to the end of the road. They didn't pass any dwellings.

Far to the right they could see a lighted window. She said: 'That's the Casson home, Eddie. Down there. Alex will have to come this way.'

At the top of the road she turned right for about a hundred yards. They reached a narrow path running down. She turned into this. It was not a road. It was of red clay, hardened by the sun. On each side of it rose banks, high banks, of the same substance. It was no wider than six feet. The walls were about eight feet high.

'Ideal, isn't it?' she murmured, switching off the motor.

They sat without speaking. Eddie was fighting an impulse to wrench the wheel from her, to stop her carrying through her diabolical scheme. But he didn't move.

Sylvia didn't betray any signs of wishing to retreat. Her face was taut and hard in the glow of the dashboard light. The green bulb cast a weird shadow under her eyes. At that moment she looked like some fantastic character from a nightmare. She said: 'He should be here at any minute.'

'Hadn't we better cut the headlamps?'

'No. He won't suspect anything. He'll be grateful for their light to see his way by. He'll think some necking couple have parked up here, out of the way.'

Eddie looked along the white swath the lamps made in the darkness of the pathway. He tensed. Down below, beyond the radius of the light, he thought he saw a shadow stir.

Sylvia saw it, too. 'There he is!'

'Think again — before it's too late!' begged Eddie, his throat suddenly dry. 'You can't do it — '

Sylvia didn't bother to answer; her grip on the brake tightened.

The trudging figure came onwards. Now they could see the dark coat, the black bag. And, indistinctly, the face . . .

'*For God's sake, Sylvia —* '

'Hang on to your hat, Eddie! *Here it is!*'

He stiffened in his seat as she threw the brake off. The ebb of the engine rose and roared. The car sprang forward like a malevolent monster of the shades. It brought the trudging man to a halt.

He stared up towards it. Then a torch flashed out, held in his right hand. He was making sure he had been seen.

Now he moved to the side of the clay bank, giving the car room to clear. He stood there, pushing back into the clay.

Nearer and nearer rushed the car. Sylvia sat at the wheel, tight and unswerving. She held the car to its course. The man ahead began to realize the car was heading straight down on to him. His mouth opened in a soundless yell, lost in the roaring throb of the engines.

Eddie's arm shot over his eyes as the Doctor whirled down before the flying wheels. He felt the savage, jarring bump, felt the car swerve madly as Sylvia momentarily lost her grip of the wheel;

then they were slowing down, slowing to a stop.

Eddie couldn't stir. Sylvia said: 'Wait here.'

She climbed out and left him. He knew she was trudging back up the hill — trudging back like a ghoul, to see if the job had been done properly!

He sat rigid, unnerved completely. All the arguing he had done with himself about it being either him or Alex, didn't lessen the horror of the reality he had just been a party to.

He was aware of nothing until Sylvia dropped into the driving seat and said: 'He's dead.'

'Was it — quick?'

'Very quick. He fell with his head under the offside wheel.' She started the car again. She didn't take the road up the hill going back, and Eddie was glad of that; he had been afraid of passing that huddled, grotesque figure, lying there by the side of the steep bank.

Twenty minutes later they arrived back at the spot where they had changed the tires. Eddie got out and started working again. So far they hadn't exchanged more than a dozen words. But now he said: 'What happens — after we've — done away with the tires?'

'I get back home as soon as I can. You go back to your hotel in Midvale and try to look as if nothing out of the ordinary has happened.'

'Go back to *Midvale?* But you said — '

'Don't be a fool. You couldn't possibly come back with me tonight.'

'When can I come back?'

'Tomorrow. To save any scandal, Alex told folks who asked where you were that you'd gone East, visiting relatives for a time. Later he was going to tell them, if they asked, that you just didn't come back again. Now you *are* coming back. And get a couple of cases. Try and seem as if you have just come back from a long journey.'

'Tomorrow,' he whispered.

'Try to make up some convincing story in case anyone does ask you where you've been. I don't think they will — but — in case.'

'I can do that. And then?'

'You stay at my place again. We'll have it to ourselves this time.'

'Won't the villagers think it's funny?'

'Why *should* they? Nothing unusual in a widow living alone, retaining the services of a general handyman, is there?'

'I — I suppose not.'

'Then it's settled, Eddie. And in case anyone happens to be there when you arrive, for heaven's sake try to remember to look suitably startled when I tell you in my finest, tearful tones, that Alex has met with — an accident.'

'I won't forget to act the part.' He finished changing the tires. They got into the car again. He asked: 'Are you certain we've removed all traces?'

'Certain. I particularly looked at the front of the car. It isn't scraped or dented in any way. The only blood was on the tires you changed.'

The horror he had been feeling was beginning to wear off now. Her matter-of-fact tone was having its effect.

'Make it about six before you get back,' she told him. 'That'll give things a chance to quiet down. They may not discover the body until morning.'

They reached the road up to the hill again. Again she swung the car along, and up past the lane where they had — killed Alex. On and upwards to the very summit of the district, where there was no foliage, and only rocks and thick patches of clay.

She halted the car in front of a small, dark crevice in the face of a jutting heap of rock. 'Get the tires, Eddie — wake up! The *tires*.'

He came back from his reverie and moved to the rumble. He lifted the lid and took the tires out one by one. Sylvia lit a torch and indicated the cave mouth. 'In there.'

He carried the tires, two in each hand, and thrust through the narrow opening into the cave. Sylvia shone the torch down on to the center of the floor.

'There it is. Drop them in, Eddie.'

The hole in the cave floor was crater-shaped. It had a raised rim, like a piecrust, of about four inches. He laid down the tires and attempted to peer down.

Sylvia came towards him and he had a

sudden feeling of insecurity. He realized he would *always* have that with *her*. He would never know the second she might take it into her pretty head to send him the way of Schaparelli and Alex.

He rose hastily. 'Looks a long way down.'

'It is. Drop in the tires and listen for them landing.'

He eased one over the hole and released it. He started to count. 'Three — four — five — six — seven — eight — nine — ' There was a scarcely audible thud. 'Nine seconds, near enough,' he mused.

'They'll never be found there.' She smiled. 'If they are, they won't necessarily be associated with Alex's death.'

'I hope not.'

She went on: 'I'll have to get back now. I'll run you as far as the Midvale road. You'll have to walk the remainder of the way.'

'Can't you take me to where you picked me up?'

'No, Eddie. I must get back as soon as I can. It's going to take me some time, because I'll have to return by a circular route. I can't risk anyone in the village seeing or hearing the car coming back at this time. That would destroy my story that I stayed in all the time from nine onwards.' He saw the sense in that, and didn't argue.

She drove back recklessly until they reached the main road to Midvale. Here she pulled up. 'This is as far as you go. It's a long walk. Perhaps you can thumb a ride. There are generally plenty of trucks rolling at night.'

He gripped her shoulder and half turned her in her seat. 'You aren't thinking of — double-crossing me, are you?'

'Of course I'm not. What made you think that?'

'I'm just warning you not to try anything like that. If you did — '

'Why talk foolishly, Eddie? I'm doing all this so we can be together, aren't I?'

'That's so. But one of these days you may get fed up with *me*! And then you may try your tricks out — only with me as victim instead of accomplice.'

'I wouldn't do anything to harm you, darling,' she said. She pulled him towards her by his shoulders and pressed her lips full to his. But somehow they lacked the power to stir him tonight . . . perhaps he hadn't ever really expected her to carry out her threat and kill Alex. It was done now, anyway.

He broke away. 'I'll go. You'd better get back in a hurry.'

'I better, hadn't I? Everything's gone all right. There isn't a clue anyone could find. I'll play my part. You take care to play yours well, when you arrive tomorrow night.'

'I'll feel easier by then.'

She kissed him again, then started the engine.

The car turned and roared back towards Garwood, leaving Eddie to thumb his way to Midvale.

★ ★ ★

He remembered walking up that dusty road before. How long ago had that been? To him it seemed like centuries, although it was just over a year. So much had happened that he hated himself for, and hated her for even more. But there was no way out. He had tried breaking it up, only to return each time. Would she always be there, throughout the rest of his life, leading him into acts at the thought of which his very soul shriveled? Or would it be different now that Alex was gone?

The things he loathed about her jumped to the front of his mind. Her obvious awareness of the spell she had cast over him. Her sneering curl of the lips; her acid remarks about his personal courage. Her scornful glance when he expressed any fears of his own.

But then there were the myriad things he felt he could never live without. They jostled each other in his mind so that even then he knew again the thrill her presence would bring him. Her soft red lips, her firm young body lying alongside his hard frame; the sympathetic understanding she could infuse into her voice if she felt that way. He loved that, even though he knew it was an act.

It was a *good* act.

Garwood came into sight and he paused irresolutely. At length he turned off into the wood, past the still pool, up through the leafy trees towards the Webster home, halfway up the rise.

She would be waiting for him. Not for the first time, he wondered if she'd been a clever enough actress to carry the thing off without betraying herself.

He came out onto the road, in front of the house. The sickening realization that only last night a happy, living man who had once befriended and helped him had walked down that path to his doom, struck him. And he, Eddie, had helped to take that life.

He pulled himself together. This wasn't the frame of mind that would present to the world a face free of guilt or guile. He opened the gate and walked up the path. The door was closed. The garage door was open and he could see the bonnet of the car in there. He shuddered again.

He rang the bell, keeping his thumb on the push. Someone started down the hall almost at once. Steps stopped at the door, the Yale was turned . . .

'Hello there.' He felt his heart thumping. It was the sheriff of Garwood!

Then he saw Sylvia behind the sheriff. She had donned a black dress, but even in plain black she managed to look the personification of freshness and youth. He was amazed at the wan, pallid appearance of her features. Undoubtedly she was a miraculous actress. She looked precisely like a woman who had heard she had lost the most priceless possession in her life.

Eddie said: 'Hello, Sheriff.'

'You know I'm sheriff here?'

'Sure. That star on your vest.'

'Oh, I see. I figured we hadn't met. You'll be Martin, the chauffeur, won't you?'

'That's me.'

'Mrs. Webster was tellin' me how you'd gone East to visit your folks. There's been a nasty bit of work here . . . '

Eddie fought to appear calm. 'Nasty — *work?* I don't get it, Sheriff.'

The sheriff lowered his voice: 'Watch what you say. Doc Webster's met a nasty end — last night. The missus is feelin' it

310

pretty bad, I guess.'

Sylvia had arrived at the door now. She said: 'Oh, Eddie. Come in.'

'I was just tellin' him about the doc,' said the sheriff.

Eddie was trying to look suitably startled, but the sheriff was not paying him much attention. He said: 'It's a good job your man arrived back today, Mrs. Webster. Now you'll have someone to see to you tonight. You need a man to look after a house as isolated as this one is. I was goin' to offer to stay here tonight until you come to some arrangements, but it seems like I won't need to now. I sure am sorry about it, Mrs. Webster. If I can do anythin' . . . Gosh, it was a cruel trick for to happen to the doc, and him so kind. Only yesterday mornin' he was orderin' more chickens from me . . . ' He put his hat on. 'I reckon I may as well be goin'. You sure about — about the body? You sure you don't want it bringing up here?'

'No — no, Sheriff. If you don't mind — having it. I couldn't stand to see poor Alex like that. I'd go mad.'

'I know how it is. The village folks is collectin' for a wreath. I guess they don't know what they're goin' to do without the doc around, either. Well . . . '

'You've been very kind, Sheriff. Thank you so much.' She held her tiny wisp of handkerchief to her eyes, and the sheriff, with a sorrowful shake of his head to Eddie, passed through the door. Eddie closed it. Sylvia lowered the handkerchief.

'Thank God you've come. These fools have been popping up to sympathize all day long.'

'Everything all right, then?'

'I told you it would be, didn't I? They found him at six this morning. Some farm workers. Sheriff Rudge had him taken to his home. Then he came up here to tell me.'

'Didn't he wonder why you hadn't worried about Alex being out all night?'

'No. I told him that Alex had gone out late, telling me he had to see a patient and might be out the night. He accepted the explanation; didn't even ask who the patient was. He takes the view it was the work of a hit-and-run driver.'

'Will there be any inquest?'

'I expect there will. A local one. They'll look for the car with tires matching the impressions they found in the dust. They won't find it.'

'How about your footprints? You walked up there.'

'I kept to the hard part of the lane, in the center. Everything will pass off smoothly now. And here we are . . . '

Eddie said: 'Yes, we are, aren't we?'

'For the time being you'll keep your old room on as a blind — just in case anyone *does* nose about. Actually you'll sleep with me.'

She moved close to him, the black material of her dress pulling taut against her figure as she clasped her arms behind his neck. She strained against him. 'Aren't you glad, Eddie? Now?'

'I guess I am — now.'

'It's so simple. And we're together and richer by seventy thousand dollars.'

He glanced uneasily about him. 'I'll be glad when we get out of this place, though. It gives me the creeps. I've got the feeling Doc is watching from every corner, Annie snooping through every window.'

'It makes *me* feel like that, too. I thought it wouldn't but it does. We'll go soon, but not *too* soon. We can't afford to rouse suspicions by running out almost immediately. Give things time to settle down.' She paused, then added: 'Go and put your bags in your room. I think we'll go to bed early tonight.'

★ ★ ★

Once again summer hurried into autumn, then to winter. And Eddie and Sylvia were still there, still together, growing surer of themselves and surfeited with their passions and emotions. Many times Eddie had asked when they were moving to the city, and always Sylvia found some excuse.

Eddie himself was pale and drawn these days. The memory of that last night when they had run down Alex he could not erase entirely from his mind. At nights, many nights, whilst Sylvia's regular breathing continued beside him, he would lie

314

awake, staring into the silence of the room and seeing the doctor's strained, anguished face at the moment of impact, reliving those moments as the car jolted cruelly over the body and rushed onward.

Nor could he understand Sylvia. He knew she hated the village in general and this house in particular. But she seemed remarkably satisfied to remain here and let things slide. Alex's money had not yet been touched. It still reposed in the bank.

She had given him the 'wanted' circular on which his name and photograph had appeared. He had burned it, every last scrap.

He found no *fault* with Sylvia. The hard side of her nature had vanished with the killing of Webster. Whether it was another of her acts he was uncertain. But she was tender and sympathetic with him now, and seemed to have troubles of her own.

These she contrived to keep well to herself, until one night towards Thanksgiving. Then she cornered him in the library. She sat on his knee before the log fire, and draped her arms about his neck.

Outside, the wind whined through the leafless trees and the cold was intense.

'Eddie . . . I'm worried.'

'About us?'

'No. About — I don't know. This place.'

'Then why don't we move?'

She shrugged. 'Because there's something to attend to first. I keep putting it off — but it *must* be done. And I need *your* help again.'

'Not anything like — *last* time?'

'No. But until it's done I won't enjoy any peace of mind. It's — *Annie*!'

'Annie?'

'Yes. I — I keep having an unpleasant sensation that she's watching, prying, snooping, like she used to do. I keep imagining I can see her — at windows, or hear her moving about in her room.'

'That's silly. Annie left here. No reason why she should come back now. Unless, of course, she heard about Alex.'

'She *won't* come back. I'm sure of that. But I can't stop myself imagining these things. We haven't *finished* with Annie.'

'Then let's go where Annie won't

worry you. It's the associations she had with this place; and once we leave it we'll *both* feel better.'

'That's my idea. I want to leave . . . '

'Then what's holding us up?'

'The thing I told you about. The thing that has to be done. Eddie — I've been — bad. Wicked. You know that yourself. You helped me — I drove you into it. But, believe me, I've changed now. You must believe that. I *have* changed, Eddie. Surely you can see it?'

'You've been different since we've been together,' he said.

'Then help me just once more. Help me to drive this — this spectre of Annie away. Once I know Annie's safely dealt with I'll come away with you. We'll leave this place forever. Will you help me just this once more?'

'Help you to — what?'

'To drag Annie from the pool and throw her down the shaft in the cave.'

14

Eddie threw her roughly from his knee and came to his feet.

'What the hell are you *talking* about, Sylvia? *Annie* — in the *pool?*'

She faced him. 'I mean what I say — Annie's in the pool. Her cases are with her, packed with her belongings. She's weighted with two large rocks tied to her neck and feet with strong rope. But the rope'll rot, Eddie . . . that's why I daren't leave here. I keep slipping down to — to see if the body's floated up. When the rope rots, it will, won't it, Eddie?'

He said: 'Then — you did that? To *Annie?* And pretended she left. How about the note?'

'I wrote that, too. That was why I told you to go up and see if you could help Alex that night. While I got rid of — Annie.'

'You murderous bitch,' he hissed. 'I could see your reason for getting rid of

Schaparelli. And I knew how you felt about Alex. But why Annie? What good did it do you to kill *her*?'

'I had to — don't you see? She saw us that night. She'd have told Alex — '

'You said he wouldn't believe her if she did.'

'But he *might*. I couldn't afford to take the chance. And I hated her prying and snooping — I did it for *us*, Eddie!'

He snapped: 'I understand one thing; that murder's deep down inside you. I believe you like killing people!'

'Only if it's necessary.'

'How did you kill her?'

'I caught her in her room, just getting back into bed. I — strangled her. It was all I could think of. She screamed, but there wasn't anyone to hear. Then I packed her bags, scrawled the note, dragged her out to the shed and pushed her into an old sack. I tied the top with some rope which I'd taken along with me. I pulled her out into the woods and down to the pool. I fastened two heavy lumps of rock to the sack and threw it in. I didn't think then that the rope would rot and the air that might be in her lungs would bring her to the top. But I've been worried crazy since, wondering when and if she *will* bob up. That's why I daren't leave. That's what has to be done before we do leave. And you'll have to help me to do it. Now — tonight! We'll take her to the crater in the cave — down there she'll never be found!'

He forced himself to speak calmly. 'I suppose it's the only way,' he said. 'You're right about not leaving until she's definitely right out of the way.'

'Then you will come with me?'

'I have to, haven't I?' he snapped savagely. 'I'm in too deep now to take any chances of you being caught out. Yes, I'll come.'

It was dark and cold outside. The trees bent like black skeletons in the pressure of the howling winds that blew across Garwood. The top window shutter creaked dismally after them as they turned out of the gates and across to the woods. The dead foliage wrapped sinuous, dank fingers about their legs, soaking them.

They gained the pool at last, and stood gazing into it.

'Just where did you throw the body?'

'At the top end, in a sort of little harbor. It was safest there. The trees overhang the water and swimmers don't use that end of the pool.'

'How deep is it?' he wanted to know.

'About fifteen feet.'

She led him round the pool to it. He stared down at the black inkiness of the water at that spot. 'How do we hook it out? We've only brought a length of rope.'

She said: 'I'll dive. I know where to look.'

He said: '*I'll* dive. You stay here — '

'Let me, Eddie. There're weeds under here — growing out from the bank. I'm used to them, you're not.'

She was slipping out of her clothes while she spoke, and now she stood naked on the edge of the pool, her hair tossed about her shoulders by the wind, her arms raised, her lithe, supple body a white fantasy in the darkness.

She was as he had first seen her; and again he felt an overwhelming surge of desire, even then, even after what he knew about her.

'Give me the rope, Eddie.'

Wordlessly he handed her the end of the rope they had brought. She leaned forward and entered the pool with hardly a splash. He waited anxiously on the bank.

The slack of the rope twisted from his loose hold as she dived down into the water . . . it stopped.

Within a few more seconds she was in view again, dashing water from her hair and eyes.

'Can't you locate her?'

'I have located her. I ran the slipknot round the end of the sack. I'll come out and help you to haul her in.'

She came out, dried herself on her slip, and then donned the rest of her dry underclothes and dress. She appeared not to be affected by the intense cold. Together they bent to the task of pulling Annie and her bags and the rocks from the bottom of the pool. In few minutes she lay before them on the bank, rendered shapeless by the waterlogged, rotting sack.

Eddie said: 'Just in time. Few more months and those ropes would have rotted through, strong as they are.'

There was a shocking odor from the corpse. Eddie fought not to let his thoughts dwell on the sliminess that must be inside the sack. He opened up the clean sack they had brought.

'In here — cut the rocks from her first.'

Sylvia obeyed quickly. She was unperturbed by the smell or by the clammy wetness of the sack and its contents. She bent, the wind whipping her dress about her, and threw the rocks back into the pool.

'All right, Eddie.'

'It's going to be tough work carrying her up to the cave,' he said. 'But we'd better do it now.'

She nodded and gripped one end of the clean sack. The cases had been stuffed inside, with Annie.

They walked through the woods, upwards, the sack swinging between them, heavy and waterlogged. Sylvia seemed not to feel the strain. She walked with far more ease than Eddie.

Out there with the wind streaming her hair out behind her, tearing at her dress and coat, she looked like some wild, sinister thing of the woods. No longer did Eddie see her as she usually looked — calm, sweet, innocent. She seemed to change with her setting. This was the setting to which she *belonged*: the dark, tempestuous night, and the evil it held hidden in the shadows of the skeletal trees which reached out clawing talons of branches towards her.

He could not see her features, but he knew the look he would have found there — defiant, triumphant, glowing and ominous. A look of the night itself. But he still wanted her!

He himself was anxious only to get the thing over with. Already the nightmare past haunted him, causing him to toss and turn wakefully and restlessly in his bed at night. Here was one more specter to add to the grisly troupe — Annie! Now she would join the gibbering, mocking cadavers that floated in ghastly array before his sleepless eyes at nights. Now she would gibber and gloat with them, robbing him of yet more peace of mind.

He had obtained some consolation from the fact that Sylvia had seemed worried, too. She had *slept* — but her face had shown the strain of *something*. But he was robbed of that . . . now he knew her fear had been of Annie rising to the top of the pool — a very real fear of discovery, not a phantasm of the mind.

Henceforth, with Annie disposed of for good, Sylvia would rest soundly. He would be alone with his own little world of nightmares. He was grateful they would be leaving tomorrow. One more night in this district, he felt, would send him half crazy.

They were out of the woods now and on the rocky trail up to the cave. There was not much farther to go — Sylvia was moving quicker every minute, as if anxious herself to get rid of that ghastly burden.

'Round the next bend,' she said.

Eddie's sigh of relief was whipped away into nothingness by the raging wind that blew up there. The cave mouth loomed before them, a darker circle of gloom in the darkness of the rock face.

'Let go, Eddie. I'll drag her through.' She entered the cave, pulling Annie, and he followed her. It was pitch black in there, until he pulled out the torch from the pocket of the greatcoat that had once belonged to Doctor Webster. He thumbed the switch and a powerful beam of light shot over the cave roof. He directed it about until the dark aperture in the floor of the cave was revealed. The torch beam spotlighted it in a glare of white. He set the torch down on a convenient piece of rock, the light splaying out about the hole.

Sylvia had laid Annie down beside the hole. Now she passed her hand across her head. 'I thought we'd be blown away before we made it,' she said. She fumbled in her coat pocket, then produced cigarettes. 'I think we deserve a smoke before we pass on to the final act in the night's grisly play.'

He lit hers and then his, with a lighter that had once been a gift from Sylvia to her husband.

'Sylvia — this is the *last* time I'm

helping you — in anything!' he told her. 'From now on, if you get into any scrapes, you get yourself out of them.'

'I won't ask you to help me any more, Eddie,' she said. There was a peculiar tone to her voice, which he missed.

He blew smoke into the cold air. 'Are we dropping — her — down, just like this?'

'Why not?'

He said uneasily: 'Maybe we ought to say a prayer . . . '

Her laughter rang round the cave, a thing of evil. 'You fool, Eddie! A *prayer*!'

He shut up. It did sound fantastic, to say a prayer over the body of the woman whose murder he was conspiring to conceal.

'May as well get on with it.'

Eddie nodded. 'Once this is done, you're certain there's nothing to hold us here? We can move then?'

'Tomorrow, first thing.' She smiled. That peculiar note was in her voice again.

Still he missed it. He wasn't thinking of anything now but getting Annie down that pit where she'd be safe from discovery. He caught hold of the sack and began to drag it towards the hole. Sylvia relaxed against the wall, watching him, smoke trickling from her nostrils. The mouth of the pit was in front of him, and gazing down into its forbidding depths he shivered, and not with the cold. What a filthy end for anyone, he thought, dead or alive.

He heaved the sack over the low ridge that ran about the hole. He pushed . . .

He watched, fascinated. The sack seemed to be floating down into the well, slowly, *slowly* . . . minutes seemed to pass before it vanished from sight. And then he listened for the thud. It came at last — faint, barely sounding above the wild cry of the wind in the cave mouth.

And simultaneously, he heard another sound: the sound of a soft step behind him . . . *on top of him.*

Some seventh sense sent him spinning round to grab crazily at Sylvia's legs as her hands thudded savagely against his bent shoulders.

A second more and he would have followed Annie. But even as the top half of his body lurched out and over, his clawing fingers found an anchorage on her knees, and he pulled himself madly back from the open shaft. Her fists rained down on his head; her pointed shoe smashed into his teeth. He was on his knees, holding her legs tightly. Her hands were against his shoulders, straining him backwards. He caught a glimpse of her face, and breath whistled from his blood-filled mouth. He felt a pulse of fear hammering at his heart.

Her face was devilish, murderous. Her even teeth gleamed in the glow of the torch; her lips were curled back from them. Her green eyes were pools of savagery . . .

'You fool! Do you think I'd let *you* live? You're going with Annie!'

He panted: 'You're mad! Let me get up — !'

She didn't speak again. Her entire strength was exerted in straining to force him over the edge. He felt his feet going over the crumbling side of the hole. Desperately, he fought back. His hand found leverage further up her legs and his nails sunk into the fleshiness of her thighs.

She forced again at his shoulders. He felt his hold on her legs loosening. His hands started to come away, nails raking long strips of flesh.

He could not hold on any longer. He was in too disadvantageous a position to gain any ground. And he was losing what he held. On impulse he threw himself violently to one side, just as she sent her full weight against him.

Her hands slipped from his shoulders. Her feet caught against the six-inch ridge — he was aware, dazedly, of seeing her body plunge downwards, past him, towards the hole . . .

He himself was safe. The grip was gone from his shoulders. He lay panting, feet still over the pit. He rolled clear and climbed painfully to his knees.

Then he saw her; he had been prepared to fight for it again. There was no need. She was down the pit — only her head and arms were visible. Her hands were clutching despairingly at the ridge she had tripped over. Her arms were taut with strain.

She sobbed: 'Eddie — Eddie — get — me — up!'

Still dazed, he rose to his feet and began to bend forward to grip her hands. Then he stopped, suddenly.

'Eddie,' she panted, her eyes staring out of her head. 'Hurry, Eddie. I can't — my fingers — *slipping* — ' Her voice rose in a thin, terrified scream.

He stood looking at her. Then he said: 'So that was why you couldn't leave Garwood? Annie — yes. But me, too! You wanted *me* out of the way! You never gave a damn for me. You just used me as long as you needed me. Now all you want is the money, damn you! And you were going to kill *me*! That's why you brought me up here with you — you wanted help with Annie, but more than that you wanted to finish me off, too. Then you could have left Garwood. They'd have thought I'd left with you — and — I'd have been down — there. With Annie!'

'No, Eddie, I didn't mean to harm you. I don't know what came over me . . . I couldn't help it. Eddie, you've got to help

331

me this time! My arms — I can't hold on here — Eddie, Eddie, Eddie . . . I love you — '

He spoke in a dull monotone. 'This is one time I haven't *got* to help you. This is one time I can walk out on you . . . because there won't be anything to come back to!'

She scrabbled desperately at the ridge, trying to draw herself up a little, and ease the pull on her shoulders. She gained a couple of inches, then her aching muscles relaxed and she jerked to the full length of her arms.

Her voice was a hoarse whisper when she spoke again. 'You can't let me die here, Eddie. You *can't*. Just help me this once more. Just this once. Eddie — we'll be together — always — '

'No!' He backed towards the cave mouth. 'No! Not this time or ever again, Sylvia!'

Her voice came in a shriek again: 'Eddie — you'll go mad when I'm not here — when you know you let me die! I don't want — to die. *Help me* . . . '

He was at the cave door. Fighting

against his impulse to help her. 'Goodbye, Sylvia.' Abruptly, he turned his back.

Her voice changed suddenly. Now it was low and venomous. 'All right, Eddie, walk out. But you won't ever get *any* rest. The things you've done — the things you helped me to do — they'll haunt you, drive you mad. With me you might have forgotten. Without me you never will. Your life will be a living hell. Until one day you'll snap and take an easy way out. *You'll never get rid of me!* I'll be there *in your mind*, Eddie! You *can* kill yourself — your body can die — but your mind *won't*. And wherever it is I'll still be there — look at me . . . for the *last time* — !'

Slowly, against his will, he turned.

Her fingertips still clung tenaciously to the ridge of rock. But her white, taut face had almost vanished beneath the lip of the hole. Her damp hair framed her pallid whiteness, and her green eyes were alive with fear and hate.

'There's still time . . . now. Hurry, Eddie!' Her fingers slipped another fraction of an inch.

'I'll never help you again,' he said mechanically.

The curses she hurled at him then were terrible to hear, more so coming from her lips as she hung suspended there with a bone-shattering death below her. Foul words he had not expected her to know poured out at him in torrents of hatred; obscene curses flayed his mind and heart.

The flood turned into a trickle, and suddenly she was sobbing. Sobs — every one of which raked his soul. But resolutely, he moved towards the cave mouth again.

'Eddie — !' The word suddenly tailed away into a high, thin echoing scream . . .

'Hold on, Sylvia, I'm coming — !' he yelled, spinning about and racing for the pit mouth. Then he stopped.

The hands were gone. The arms were gone. The face was gone.

And back from the pit came a long, shuddering scream, growing fainter and fainter.

Momentarily it stopped. And he was at the pit mouth when it was renewed again; but now they were screams of terrible agony, rising up from the bowels of the earth as if the mouth of Hades had opened up and was releasing the tormented shrieks of its burning victims.

On and on went the screams; and, cold and stiff, Eddie stared down into the blackness. Once he cried:

'Sylvia — Sylvia . . . Oh, Christ — *Sylvia*!' Tears coursed freely down his cheeks, rolled from his skin and fell into the pit. But his voice was drowned by those anguished cries . . .

He did not know how long he was there. It seemed a century. But finally the screams became moans, moans of a person in the last extremities of pain and suffering; and then these, too, died, and there was nothing other than the wailing of the wind outside and the broken sound of Eddie's sobs.

Dawn was creeping into the cave when he rose and stood upright. His face was expressionless, a mask held steady by his broken mind. Staring unseeingly ahead, he walked towards the cave mouth again. His shoe ground down on a cigarette end smeared with lipstick.

Then he was outside.

He did not return to the Webster home. The full morning found him trudging laboriously along the road to Midvale, hollow-eyed and stoop-shouldered, a man with a mind dangerously near snapping point.

Once a truck driver stopped and yelled: 'Wanna lift, bud?' but Eddie seemed not to hear him. He tramped on . . .

★ ★ ★

The very scent of spring was abroad. Fresh shoots were bursting from wintry branches, and birds were welcoming the return of the milder weather.

The Chicago passenger loco chugged steadily along on its course. At the back there was a freight car, doors partly opened to admit the warm sun. Inside were two men: a sallow, shriveled-looking hobo, and a larger man, eating fried chicken. How he'd come by it was his secret. But he was generous to his fellows in misfortune.

'Yuh wanta have a chew on this here

leg, son? Yuh sure look hungry.'

The other seemed to be busy with his thoughts. But he raised his head and regarded his companion with hollow eyes that seemed to stare right through him.

'Yuh feel all right, son? Yuh looks mighty poorly!'

'I'm okay. I guess I could eat some of that chicken.'

The big man handed over a generous leg. 'Git goin' on that. How far yuh ridin' on this here loco?'

'I guess I don't know.'

'Yuh don't know?'

'No. I got troubles.'

The big man chuckled. 'Whoever heard o' a bum havin' troubles!'

'Well I got 'em. Where's the train headin'?'

'Chicago.'

The other nodded. 'Then I guess that's where I'm goin'. I seem to have been everyplace else.'

The train rattled on.

★   ★   ★

The concrete paths of the park were hot from the long day of sunlight. The cop was walking leisurely under the leafy trees, past trim beds of flowers. In a few minutes the park would close its gates, and the cop was taking a last look round. It was a part of his job.

He cut across the grass to a shady seat under a tree. There was a bum there with his chin sunk on his chest. His chin and cheeks were thick with stubble. His hat was canted over his eyes. He seemed to be mumbling to himself in his sleep.

The cop prodded him with an unsympathetic nightstick.

'Hey! Wake up — '

The hobo jumped and looked up. For a second a hint of fear showed in his expressionless face. 'I wasn't asleep, officer.'

'That don't matter; you can't sit there all night. On your way.'

The hobo got up and walked away. The cop muttered to himself: 'I sure wouldn't like to have the load on my mind that that guy seems to have.'

★　★　★

338

The line of men tramped steadily on to the ship by one plank and off by another. They carried out sides of ham and loaded them into the warehouse alongside. Amongst them was a man with a lined, worn face. His eyes were sunken deep into his skull. He worked automatically. The burly, red-faced ganger by the outgoing plank called him over.

'When'd you start here?'

'Yesterday afternoon.'

'Well this mornin' you quit. Pick up what's due to you on your way out. An' if you want to hold a job down stop walkin' round like a character in a dream.'

The man said: 'You mean nightmare.'

'Huh?'

'Give me another chance. I didn't sleep last night. I never sleep so good . . . Maybe the work'll help me . . . '

The ganger said: 'It's a doctor you want if you don't sleep.'

'A doctor couldn't do me no good.'

'You say so. Anyhow, you ain't got it in you to do this kinda work. If I was you, I'd try get myself somethin' lighter — mebbe a job as a janitor.'

The man drooped even more, and without another word shuffled away towards the dock gates.

★   ★   ★

The doss house was along the Bowery. A motley crowd of down-and-outs thronged into it every night from nearby soup kitchens. They paid ten cents a night, and according to how tough they were they either got a rough wooden trestle with a straw-filled mattress, liberally occupied by fleas, or the floor.

The staring man got the floor. He lay down, his shabby suit hanging loosely against his bony, worn-out frame. It was cold, and the patrons of the doss house huddled together against it. They slept, filling the room with rumbling, grunting, and whistling. At one end a wizened old hobo went cautiously through the pockets of those near him.

The entire room came to wakefulness suddenly. The staring man in the corner was screaming continuously in his sleep,

screaming words that were indistinguish-
able.

'Quit that row!'

'Pipe down there, you nut!'

'What's wrong with that bastard? Give
him a kick.'

Someone obliged. The screaming man
woke suddenly.

'What's eating you? You're screechin' fit
to bust your pants.'

He mumbled: 'I'm sorry — I guess I
don't — sleep so good.'

'I guess we won't, long as you're here,
either.'

'I get — nightmares.'

A wit yelled: 'Well saddle one up and
take a ride, pal.'

'Yeah, you better blow. Nobody can
sleep for that racket you're kickin' up.
Mebbe you been on the bottle too much.
I'm troubled with dee tees myself,
sometimes.'

The staring man rose and picked his
way towards the door. He went out.

The man who'd been next to him said:
'That guy's nuts. He was yellin' somethin'
that sounded like — 'Hold on, Sylvia

— don't let go. Hold on'.'

The wit grinned. 'Maybe he figgered he was with his best gal!'

★ ★ ★

It was winter. The ground was thick with white; the trees were icy patterns of lace-like branches against the full moon.

The field was some little way outside town. At one side of it was a highway; at the other, the railroad tracks. The hunched figure of a man struggled through the deep drifts towards the railroad. He was blue with cold, but he seemed not to feel it.

He reached the track and took the faded, torn photograph from his inside pocket. He sat by the tracks in the shadow of a clump of trees and peered at the girl's face smiling out at him. He mumbled, between chattering teeth: 'I guess you were right. I can't get any peace anymore. I guess you were right.'

Round the bend of the track a loco came hurtling. The whistle shrilled on the frosty air. The man rose, went on to the

342

tracks, and lay across them where the trees made deep shadows. The photograph was tightly clutched in his right hand. The chill of the rails paralyzed his neck muscles. The train was nearer. He could feel the track under his neck and legs trembling with its weight; could hear the rumble of it thrown up from the snowy ground.

It came screaming down on him out of the night, sparks flying from the cab . . .

★   ★   ★

The morgue attendant said: 'This is him. Pretty neat job. Face wasn't touched. The guy looks like he hasn't slept for a year!'

'Suicide?'

'Nothin' else but.'

The man from headquarters said: 'Anything on him?'

'Nothin' in his pockets. He had this clutched tight in one hand.'

'Hmm. Swell-looking girl. Maybe his sister — maybe his girlfriend. Who knows? Nothin' else?'

The morgue keeper said: 'No — oh,

wait a minute. The cop who went over him when he was brought in found one other thing.' He held up a cigarette stained with lipstick, which was still visible through a coating of grime. 'This seemed to have slipped through a hole in the linin' of his jacket. Doesn't mean anythin', I don't suppose?'

'Not a thing. A smoke smeared with lip-juice? What could a thing like that have to do with a hobo committing suicide? Most likely he picked that one up from the gutter. Any tags on his clothes?'

'There had been — they'd all been cut off.'

The man from headquarters turned back the sheet over the still figure on the ice-tray. He said: 'You're right. The guy looks like he hasn't slept for a century, never mind a year.'

And with a callousness bred in him by the constant sight of death in all its forms, the morgue attendant grinned. 'Well, he's sleepin' all right now!'

But that was only what *he* thought.

THE END